BREEDING LILACS

Alice La Roux

.

Author's Note

This novella is part of the Death Blooms world created by Yolanda Olson.

It is not rainbows and sparkly unicorns and deals with some dark topics so reader discretion is advised. What's grey for you, might be dark to others.

Kidnapping, human trafficking, forced breeding, violence, sexual situation, potential incest, non-con, dub-con, murder, being buried alive and abuse are all mentioned, some in more detail and graphic than others.

Playlist

AFI — Silver and Cold

Twenty one pilots — Chlorine

Bring Me The Horizon — Can You Feel My Heart

Fall Out Boy — The Last Of The Real Ones

Bring Me The Horizon (ft. Amy Lee) — One Day The Only Butterflies Left Will Be in Your Chest As You March Towards Your Death

Architects — Do You Dream Of Armageddon?

YUNGBLUD — hope for the underrated youth

Machine Gun Kelly — Bloody Valentine

The Offspring — You're Gonna Go Far, Kid

Broods — Bridges

Dido — Life for Rent

Amber Run —Worship

This book is for all the flowers who bloomed despite the shitty conditions they were planted in, or the careless gardeners who were supposed to help them grow.
You are still thriving.

Hope you enjoy!
Alice Le Roux
x

"April is the cruelest month, breeding
lilacs out of the dead land, mixing
memory and desire, stirring
dull roots with spring rain."
— T.S. Eliot

The Arboretum cordially invites you to attend a germination event on the 20th of October 2020.

After honing our techniques for over twenty-five years, we are proud to implement a unique system to ensure rare and luxury blooms here at The Arboretum.

From the quality of our soil to breeding the exquisite species we've specially cultivated and lovingly arranged, we take our role in the growth cycle very seriously.

As an expert in your field, we invite you, fellow horticulturists, to indulge in a weekend of innovation and collaboration in the name of science and for the beauty of creation.

- Aster Bramwell

CHAPTER ONE

Lilac

Have you ever had that feeling? The one where you wake from a nightmare, skin slick with sweat, chest heavy and tight as you struggle to catch your breath. At that moment you're sure that it's all real because no dream could ever be that convincing, that haunting, that soul-destroying? After a few moments, the remnants of the sleep haze fade, the fear dwindles and slowly you come back to your senses, and you're safe and warm in your bed. Exactly where you should be.

Except as I listen to the sound of water trickling down the wall, falling to the floor with a slow monotonous drip, as the cool air wraps itself around me, the dream state doesn't fade. It clings like a fog, no matter how many times I close my eyes and count to ten. No matter how many times I reach up and rub the sleep from my eyes. No matter how I beg and scold myself, shouting '*Wake up!*' I know it's not really a dream.

This is my new reality, and I don't understand it. I don't know how I got here or where here even is. The last thing I remember is leaving a work dinner, slightly worse for wear and trying to hail down a cab. There was a man...I think there was a man. I don't know. I can't seem to remember, my memories are just broken shards, flashes of colors and smells. Like the sickly-sweet scent of lilies lingering in the air, reminding me of funerals.

My body feels like lead, like I'm nothing more than a combination of hulking limbs, pulling me down into the mattress. The steady thumping in my head is unlike any hangover I've ever experienced and the way sensations slowly seem to be trickling back into my fingers and toes tell me that something isn't right.

I was drugged. I must have been. I'd only had two

glasses of wine, and wine didn't make you feel like this the next morning. *And then what Lila? Where are you now? Who would do this to you?* Glancing around the room, nothing is revealed. It's small, dark and damp with concrete walls and a cold stone floor. The water trickling in seems to be caused by a leak from above since there are no windows or pipes in here. I'm lying on a small cot tucked away in the corner, with a mattress that is surprisingly comfortable considering how bare the room is. My eyes snag on a steel door with bars that run the length of it, reminding me of a cage, the kind you imagine inside a prison and it feels like my heart stops as I try to breathe. Fuck. Where am I?

When I finally feel stable enough to move, I push myself up into a sitting position with great effort. It's like my arms are noodles, weak and soft as I try to support my weight. With my back against the wall, I pull my knees up to my chest and flinch when I realize my left ankle is shackled to the bed with a length of chain. My clothes are gone and instead I'm wearing some sort of cream cotton shift nightgown. Positioning myself so I can watch the door, I try to get my ragged breathing under control. *Remember. Come on Lila, remember something. Anything.*

There's nothing. Just a hollowness that settles over me. I've seen enough horror films to know that panicking is not going to get me anywhere. And I grew up inside the care system, so I know no one is going to help me—I have to help myself. To do that, I need to figure out what the heck is going on and what my options are, but I know that freaking out isn't one of them. I don't have the luxury of that. Not if I want to survive. And I want to survive. I didn't go through eighteen years of hell to just give up now, not when I was on the verge of freedom. No one was going to come looking for me because I had no one. I was alone, and I liked it that way. I finally had my own apartment, a job I liked, and at twenty-one, this was my chance to live life the way I wanted. Squeezing my eyes shut and trying one last time to wake myself from the nightmare of my life, I pinch myself and inhale slowly. When I exhale, I'm still in the small dark room, chained to a bed with no memories of how I got here.

Time passes but I'm not sure how much. I finally have full control over my body and the sluggish feeling dwindles, but now there's a gnawing in my stomach and my mouth feels like I've eaten a thousand cotton wool balls.

Standing, I shuffle towards the door, getting as close to the bars as the chain around my ankle will allow. "Hello? Is anyone out there?"

Silence.

Trying again, I manage to croak out, "Hello? Can I please get some water? Maybe something to eat?"

Finally, I hear a soft whimper somewhere down the corridor to my right. I can just see a dimly lit corridor, with several dark shapes. I think there may be other doors but with no light, I can't be sure. With the uneven walls, it feels almost like a creepy cavern rather than a building.

Another voice hisses from somewhere to my left I think, but my head is fuzzy. "Be quiet! Hush before she hears you!"

"Who? Who will hear me?" Part of me is relieved that I'm not down here alone, another part is terrified about what that means.

"Shut up!" The harsh voice growls and I realize it's female. The whimpering becomes a muffled sobbing.

Footsteps echo down the corridor, and I crawl back onto my cot. There's a lump in my throat, and my body is on high alert. I can hear my heartbeat. Deafening. *Ba-dum. Ba-dum. Ba-dum.* It's so loud, I'm almost sure that whoever is approaching can hear it too, and is using it to march towards me, their footfalls in sync with my fear.

The jangling of keys sends a tremor through me and I bite the inside of my cheek as I force myself not to cower. I hear the sound of metal scraping on stone, with hinges creaking so loud it's like I can feel it in my bones, but my door stays shut.

Slicing through the air like a whip, there's a loud cracking noise as someone cries out and once again there's silence. The sobbing stops. I bite down harder, tasting the familiar copper tang as I draw blood, fighting back the urge to call out. I suppress the need to see if the sobbing person was okay, reluctant to draw the attention of the owner of the footsteps. Survival was paramount. And if that meant I had to stay silent, if I had to let someone else suffer, then I would swallow that guilt. It could rot my soul from the inside, but later. When I got out of here, I could reflect on the way I kept my mouth shut but now wasn't the time for that.

A gentle glow creeps through the metal bars and I realize that whoever has come down to see us has a large lantern with them. It's a deliberate choice, as it still keeps everything shrouded in darkness and shadows, only illuminating the outlines of two people. The figure holding the lantern is larger and broad, towering over the smaller one. It takes me a few minutes of squinting through the hazy light and darkness to realize that it's a man and woman, but neither of them says anything as the woman pulls a small box from a bag and slips it through the bars at the bottom on my door and onto the floor. A bottle of what I assume is water follows.

"Eat." Her voice is gravelly and quiet.

I shift forward on the bed, reluctant to get too close. "Who are you? Why am I here?"

There's tension in the air as she sighs, "Eat, or we'll be forced to make you eat and you don't want that."

The man holding the lantern stands further back, and as a result I can't see the woman's features. I have no idea if she's even looking at me as the light refuses to stretch that far.

I try again, keeping my voice low since loud noises seem to be an issue. "Why am I here?"

She appears to tilt her head, "To be part of the garden of course."

A shiver runs through me, the black outlines of my captors making my chest constrict. They looked like monsters, demons lurking in the corridor, ready to devour me. "Garden?"

What madness had I woken up to? Garden? How could I be part of a garden? Were they talking about burying me?

I slide off the bed and take a hesitant step towards the door, hoping to find a way to build a rapport with the woman.

That's what they say, isn't it? Humanize yourself, that way the kidnapper will find it harder to kill you. I mean, I've listened to the podcasts and seen the tv shows but in reality, moving towards the nut job who kidnapped you is very different.

My body is screaming at me to retreat, but I can't lose this opportunity.

"Father's garden." There's another sigh and I know her patience with me is wearing thin. I can hear it in the boredom in her voice. "Lilac, eat. I won't tell you again."

I stiffen and pull back, "My name's not Lilac. It's Lila."

I may not be able to see it, but I can feel the air practically vibrate as she rolls her eyes. "That's not what your birth certificate says."

My birth certificate. I'd only recently applied for a replacement a few years ago since the original was lost in a fire when I was a child.

My birth mother had fallen asleep in our trailer, strung out and with her cigarette still lit.

It was the reason I'd ended up in the foster care system since my birth certificate wasn't the only thing that went up in flames that day.

"What?" I swallow, the motion painful since it felt like I'd swallowed glass. "Who are you?"

"We're just the nursery workers," The woman moves away from the door and straightens. "We help tend the garden. Now, this is your last chance Lilac. We can't have disobedient flowers. Trust me when I say you won't like it if I have to force you to eat."

The man behind her still says nothing, and I have no idea if he's even paying attention to our conversation since his face, like hers, is completely shrouded in shadows.

Hand trembling, I reach out and take the water and the box, opening the small container to reveal a rice and chicken dish.

It smells divine and makes my stomach growl loudly.

I use my fingers and tear the chicken breast into smaller pieces, before placing one in my mouth.

There's no cutlery provided, probably because they know that I would attempt to make a shiv out of one. Not that I've ever made a shiv in my life, but again, I'd seen enough prison dramas to give it a good go.

"It's our job to care for you, to ensure you bloom." There's a hint of satisfaction in her husky tone. "A wilted flower is no good, and Father prides himself on creating the most beautiful bouquets."

I was not a delicate flower. I wasn't going to bloom for them, wherever the fuck that meant. I don't know what their end game is, but I was a weed. I had always been a weed, at the bottom of the food chain, an inconvenience.

Three foster families had returned me, telling the social workers that I was a problem child. I didn't fit in. I wasn't like other children; I was too difficult. An irritation that couldn't be disposed of.

And if these crazies wanted to feed and water me, while I crept up amongst their crop then so be it. I was going to destroy their garden.

August

She doesn't cry. Not one tear slips from those huge violet eyes of hers. Not a single drop of pain or fear or loathing escapes.

I already knew she was different from the others. I'd known it weeks ago when Father had asked me to cultivate her. Using the last known address I could find, I'd spent days waiting in a coffee shop opposite the dilapidated block of flats, looking for a woman who matched her description. A description that it had taken me all of a day to procure after casually making conversation with her landlord, pretending to be interested in a vacant apartment two floors above hers.

For someone who didn't want to be found, she wasn't hiding very well.

Lilac had soft chocolate curls that fell around her face wildly, refusing to be tamed. Sharp cheekbones and a wary gleam gave her a harsh expression at first glance, her mouth was always drawn into a straight line as if she'd forgotten how to smile, but I'd seen it. I'd caught a glimpse of it when she'd stopped to help her elderly neighbor with some shopping, and her whole face had changed, lighting up so brightly I was almost blinded.

Why doesn't she cry? The others cried. All of them. When they finally come around and see the room, the shackle, my sister...that's when reality hits them. They don't understand. They don't see what Father is doing here when they wake, but they come around eventually.

April's voice is harsh as she reminds her to eat again. It's been two days since Lilac regained consciousness, six since we'd taken her and four since my father last examined her. He was eager to add to his garden, but as a horticulturist, he knew better than to rush.

The night I'd cultivated her she'd been out drinking with the people she worked with at a small bank. It had been easy enough to watch her from the bar, and when I saw that she was the only one drinking red wine I used the opportunity that had presented itself. I was planning on intercepting her before she made it back to her apartment, but the chance to take her before she'd even stumbled into a cab turned out to be one too delicious to turn down.

The waiter had placed the tray of drinks down on the bar while he continued preparing the order, and it was barely any effort to stretch across and drop two small pills into the ruby liquid. I love it when things fall into place, and April teases me for it, but I view it as a sign of what is meant to be. The universe was showing me that it was destiny since it was easy to pluck her from her life. It was meant to be that she fell into my arms that night. A sign that she was meant to be here with me.

Rose is sobbing again down the corridor, the sound pulling me from my thoughts of rightness and universal signs. She never learns that one, and I blame April for it. Her approach to discipline is too harsh. She is too quick to anger and that makes Rose quiet, for a short while before she cries louder when she thinks we cannot hear. But we hear everything down here.

"That damned girl," April hisses, standing from her crouched position in front of Lilac's door. "Give me the spare torch. I'll see to her; you need to make sure this one eats every mouthful."

I grab the small torch from the pouch in my hoodie. After we fed and watered the seeds, I was planning on leaving the compound to see if I could work out some of my frustration. An uneasy feeling had settled into my bones since Lilac had woken. No, since Lilac refused to cry and it was making me restless. I was hoping to tire out my body with the aim of silencing my mind along with it. Sleep never came easily here, not at The Arboretum, but we were not allowed to leave for longer than a few days at a time.

"Auggie! Make her eat." April called down the hallway before she slipped into Rose's room and the sobbing went quiet once again.

Following April's commands made my life easier, and I liked it when things were ordered and simple. It made my head quiet, and when my head was quiet Father was nicer to me.

"Auggie? Is that your name?" Lilac whispers, she never talks loudly or screams. I say nothing. Her voice is soft, and for a moment I imagine being lulled to sleep with her gentle words surrounding me.

Placing the lantern down by my feet, I hunch down into a squat. Pushing the lunchbox further into the room, I nod towards it, reminding her that she should eat and silently exhale in relief as she reaches out, fingers brushing against mine before she clasps the box to her chest and digs in.

There's no hysteria. No fight. No loudness. This one

is special. Father will make a fortune with her sprouts. The germination process will begin shortly and there's an unexpected tightness in my chest as I think about the new cultivar. The current flower arrangement promises to be one of the best, something which will please Father to no end and yet...I don't wish for him to reach the xeriscaping phase with Lilac. She's not like the others in The Greenhouse.

A scraping noise fills the air as she pushes the empty lunch box back towards me with a small smile. "That was very nice, Auggie. Thank you for taking care of me."

My jaw drops ever so slightly before I catch myself. No one has ever thanked me before, not for this.

A heavy thud fills the air, followed by a subdued groan before April emerges from the room further down the corridor, wiping bloody fingers on her dark jumper. "Eugh. August? Are you ready to leave?"

I move to push myself back onto my feet when a small hand darts out and grabs my wrist.

"Goodnight August," Lilac whispers before letting go, squinting through the darkness as though she was looking directly at me.

As I follow April down the corridor, up the stairs and towards Father's terrarium I swear I can still feel her fingers pressing into my flesh. The warmth of her touch lingers where it has no business existing.

A ster Bramwell sat at the head of the dining room table, reading his morning paper as he twiddled his greying mustache, ignoring April and me as if we were nothing more than empty air. It wasn't a new occurrence, it was simply that my father was often lost inside his own head, his genius demanding his attention whereas we were inconsequential. He once told me that we were the murmurings of his mistakes, and he had no space to dwell upon mistakes, not when his garden required his attention.

"Father, the progress with the current seeds is going well. The Lilac shows the most promise, while Poppy and Rose are developing as expected." April grins as the staff brings in our breakfast. Her smile is the mirror of his, wolfish and almost sinister and I'm struck by the way her eyes light up with this glimmer of cruelty. It wasn't that April was brutal or barbaric, she was methodical, like our father. She was interested in the results, in making him happy and the journey didn't matter, only the ending.

We'd never grown up wanting anything here at The Arboretum since our father was from a long line of botanists and horticulturists who had invested in land across the country, which paid dividends by the time my father decided to begin his little venture. The converted plantation house that had been in our family for generations was outside the city limits since the plants required space and my father required privacy. Outside the land boasted a small private vineyard, several large polytunnels and a larger nursery. The jewel in my father's crown was his greenhouse, which my great grandfather had built using a traditional Victorian glasshouse design. Underneath the house was where the current flowers were kept, in basement rooms that had been dug years ago by some distant ancestor.

"Hmmm," he grumbles, not looking at us as he folds away his paper and checks the emails on his phone. Being a leading expert on plants, he was often in discussions with botanical gardens, nurseries, vineyards and such across the world which meant he was constantly on the smart device.

April continues as she spreads strawberry jelly on her toast before scooping some scrambled eggs into her mouth. "I expect we can move onto the germinating stage shortly. Once they begin sprouting, we can transfer them into the nursery with the others."

I cut my bacon into smaller pieces, not looking up from my plate as I eat. Father is in an agitated mood, I can tell by the way his mouth turns downwards every time April talks which means that if I do something to upset him this morning, I will be punished. I don't want to spend the day dealing with deadhead flowers or grinding up the bone meal for the beds. I want to see Lilac.

After a few minutes of frowning, Father throws down his phone and snorts. "Gray has no taste, no talent! His little pets are nothing more than a cut and stick project."

My father was obsessed with another creator who was only ever whispered about in the shadows and of course, on the dark web. Gray was a thing of legends in our circles, making rare pieces that brought in thousands of dollars and I found his art to be both disturbing and yet oddly intriguing. How did he choose his creatures? How did he plan out his pieces?

"Have you been browsing the Mortality Market forum again? I don't understand why you follow his work so closely, Father." Sighing, April rolls her eyes at me and I bite back a snort. "What we're doing here is not the same, so it's not comparable."

The Mortality Market was the only safe place we could discuss our projects, network with others and make certain...purchases and sales. It was buried in the deep, dark web in order to hide from prying eyes and to find it, you had to be so entrenched in the mulch of the world that your soul was as black as tar. Of course, it's where my father listed his most beautiful blooms and any sprouts or seedlings he no longer had use for, although my father was also a man who believed in recycling so there was rarely anything that needed to be disposed of.

"Pft! Of course, it's not the same. My blooms are the best because we take the time to cultivate and germinate them with only the finest care and devotion. That's what makes the whole progress lengthy and arduous, but the payoff simply cannot be matched. And definitely not by that...butcher of a man." Angry green eyes flash across the table as he catches my gaze. I swallow, unsure of what to say as he peers at me. Under his scrutinizing glare, I squirm inside, but I'm very careful not to move. Bramwell's do not show weakness. I was already a failed creation, weakness would not be tolerated.

"I enjoy his creations," April shrugs as she passes me a piece of buttered toast, distracting our father with the motion. "There is something so very raw about them. Like he's stripped away everything they are and reduced them to their baser selves before reconstructing them as something divine."

Chuckling, Father finally pours himself a cup of coffee. "Of course you would see it like that, my little Aldrovanda. That is why you are running The Arboretum and not your deadhead of a brother."

Deadhead. It's when you remove a flower to enhance the performance of the other. Re-routing the energy and resources into the others, making them stronger at the cost of the one. The simplest method is to pinch off the faded bloom with a finger and thumb and I'm under no illusion that one day my father's hand will be on my neck in the same way.

CHAPTER TWO

Lilac

Time passes differently when there's no light and your meals are indistinguishable from one another. There is no breakfast or dinner, it's all just healthy balanced food. I think I may have been eating salmon for breakfast today, but I'm unsure since there is no way to tell.

April is still the one who brings my lunchbox and talks to me, but I can feel his eyes on me. He watches me from the shadows, like a predator, lying in wait as he stands behind her with his lantern.

Through hushed whispers I've learned that the other women down here are called Poppy and Rose, Rose is the crier who keeps getting April's undivided attention with her tears. She doesn't tell me what April does to her, but she doesn't need to. I can hear the sound of flesh slapping flesh, the thuds and thumps, the groans and swallowed screams. They echo around the corridor every day, the only soundtrack to my life right now.

Poppy is more pragmatic, trying to keep on April's good side, but she still can't make herself submit fully. She's never endured anything like this before and the urge to fight makes her do stupid things, like the last mealtime when she spat in April's face. I don't know what the punishment was, but I haven't heard from her since.

"You're the only one who doesn't give me any trouble, Lilac." Crouching before me, April's eyes look like shiny black coals in the darkness. "That makes me wary of you."

The limited light means that I still can't get a proper look at their faces, only catching snatches here and there in brief moments that the golden glow lingers on her skin. And while April is happy to talk, well, make little remarks and comments amongst the reminders to eat and 'grow', August is always silent.

"Why don't you scream? Or fight as the others do?" She rasps as she reaches through the bars to stroke my hair, twirling it between her fingers. It's greasy and unkempt since it hasn't been washed since I woke up in my tiny cell. I'm beginning to wonder if the gruffness of her voice is some sort of physical affliction rather than some sort of attempt to appear more intimidating.

Swallowing I force myself to look from her to August looming behind. "Will it make a difference?"

The fact that they were talking to me was a positive indicator. I'd learned early in life that when people wanted to hurt you, to break you, they just did it. No frills, no organic meals, no conversation. Just pain and fear. The logical part of my brain was constantly reminding me to behave, to keep my words hushed and to submit. The other part of me rebelled. I wanted to scream and cry and spit at them through the bars, but where had it gotten Rose? No, playing the long game, the survival game was the better approach. After all, a master never kept an eye on the obedient slave at his feet while overlooking his kingdom. It would be easier to let them think I was docile than to show my hand too early.

"No, but I would feel more at ease around you."

April's fingers have shifted from my hair to my face, her short nails dragging softly down my cheek before she grabs my chin and tilts my face upwards. "You're making my brother nervous with your lack of spirit."

My gaze flits to him once again and there's a nudge inside my head, something telling me that he'll be my key to escaping. I just have to figure out how to reach him.

Shrugging, I tug my face free and lower my eyes to where my hands are clasped in my lap. "I've been here before."

The ceiling dripping is the only sound before April snatches my hair, this time hurting as she tugs my head back. August seems to take a half-step forward before stopping himself and lowering the lantern, plunging us further into the world of shadows and darkness.

I can feel the air shift as I'm pulled closer to the bars, the metal cold against my cheek, and though I can't see it, I can hear the grin on her face, reminding me of a Cheshire cat. Sinister and dangerous as she growls, "Oh, I very much doubt that."

"My body has never been my own," I murmur as she moves her face alongside mine. My scalp stings as her grip tightens and she yanks my hair again. "One abusive asshole is the same as the next."

The sickly-sweet scent that lingers around April

reminds me of death. Lilies again. To my surprise, she laughs at my words. "We're here to help you reach your full potential. To see you bloom. If it hurts along the way, then that's what must happen."

Biting the inside of my cheek, I say nothing. People like her will always justify their actions somehow, I'd had enough counseling in my life to come to terms with that. It didn't matter how I reasoned with her, she thought she was helping me 'bloom'. Whatever the fuck that meant. She was just the same as the others, only this time I knew how to detach. Dissociating was something I'd learned early on in life, and I'd become so adept, I was considering adding it to my resume under the skills section. I almost laugh, I can feel it bubbling up my throat but now was not the time to indulge in my dark humor.

The pressure finally ends as she releases me, and I fall back, using my palms to steady myself.

April stands, and my skin prickles as her eyes roam over me. "Your acceptance will be rewarded, I'll talk to Father about it."

I didn't want her rewards. I wanted my freedom.

The next time April and August come, they're joined by two others, each holding lanterns. Instead of lunch boxes, they bring handcuffs with them and my heart jumps into my throat as my door opens with a whine, the hinges in desperate need of oiling.

"Sit on the bed," April commands without bothering to greet me. I was used to her short temper at this point, which sent a shiver through me since the trickle of awareness meant I was growing complacent. Complacency was dangerous, it was when mistakes were made. "I'm going to unlock your ankle cuff, and then August is going to restrain you. If you fight him, you will regret it."

I nod as I shuffle back onto the bed, my back against the wall with my feet dangling over the edge.

Her small hand grabs my ankle roughly and she pins my leg in place as she works on the lock. "I mean it, Lilac. If there's even so much as one scratch, one nail mark, anything on Auggie—I will not hesitate to kill you."

This is the first time she's directly threatened to end my life. Interesting. I file away the information for later. "I understand."

The metal cuff falls from my ankle and lands on the

floor with a loud clang, before April stands. "Good, now if only Rose was as perceptive as you."

She motions to one of the men to follow her to the left and the scream that fills the corridor moments later tells me that Rose is still resisting. I wish I had her determination, her spirit. But that's a liability, a weakness I can't afford. The break is always harsher, more brutal if you fight it.

August silently and quickly fills the space April just vacated. I hold my hands out ready for the cuffs and with a few clicks, they're in place, cool against my skin. Waiting for further instruction, I don't move, using the time to see if I can make out any more about my captor. He's broad and tall, I already knew that. The way the light casts across his profile tells me that his face is angular, sharp lines define his features.

I inhale sharply as August gets down on one knee, pulling the lantern closer to tackle a look at my bruised ankle. When he sees the marks on my pale flesh, he reaches out gently and... massages the skin. His face is now bathed in light, and I'm not prepared for the tenderness that flits across his expression.

"You don't have to do that, I'm fine," I whisper, placing my hand carefully and lightly over his which is only a little awkward with the cuffs on. He tenses under my touch, his whole body going stiff as stares at where we're connected.

Finally, he stands and motions for me to get to my feet. I do as I'm told, reminding them that I am obedient. I am well-behaved. I am no threat. Inhaling, I follow him out and down the corridor, towards a set of stone steps. I can hear voices, crying and shuffling noises in the darkness behind us as we ascend and August opens a hatch up ahead. Pulling me gently through, I don't realize I'm out in the fresh air until the breeze hits me.

Biting back a sudden sob, I push down the uproar of emotions surging through me. I missed this. I missed fresh air, and the biting cold, I missed the grass beneath my bare feet, the way it tickles and feels slick with dew. I can't make out much in the darkness, a few towering shapes that must be buildings and lots of trees. Everywhere.

Placing his hand on my elbow, August guides us towards a huge building that looks like a plantation house. The bright light burns my eyes as he lets us in the back door and it takes a while for my eyes to focus properly. I can finally see what I missed in the glow of the lantern. August's face isn't just angular, it's beautiful. But the razor-sharp, deadly kind of beautiful with a strong jawline, prominent nose and cheekbones that could slice through butter. His gaze is attentive, and I realize his eyes are a dark shade of green and not black like I'd expected. His hair is a sandy color, with a slightly red hue when it catches under the light.

He leads me into what must have previously been a utility room or mudroom of sorts, except now it's a wet room. There are three showerheads, but that's it. There are no shelves, no mirrors, nothing that could be used as a weapon or smuggled out of here for later.

A soft snipping noise makes me jump, and when I glance over my shoulder, August is cutting my nightgown from my body. Once he has the cotton in his hands and I'm completely exposed, he tosses it aside and turns one of the showers on. I don't feel embarrassed because like I'd told April, my body has never been my own. It's a shell. A skinsuit, housing all my broken parts.

Just as I'm about to get under the water, the others join us. It's strange seeing them under full lighting like this. Rose is anything but soft and delicate like her namesake, her lithe, tall frame is muscular and I wonder if she's an athlete of some kind as April begins cutting off her shift, one of the unknown men holding Rose in place. Bruises and small gashes cover her stomach, arms and thighs. I wonder how long she'd been here; how long April has been cutting into her like she was scoring a ham joint. Rose, of course, screams and the resounding crack that fills the air no longer makes me flinch like it once did. Glaring at April with a bloody lip, Rose falls silent.

Poppy shuffles in next, she's a petite woman, curvy with short blonde hair and cornflower blue eyes. The bags under her eyes tell me that she's on the verge of falling apart, the wobble of her bottom lip a sign of the tears she's holding back. There's a faint yellow bruise under her right eye, but as her nightgown is stripped away her body is free of any other blossoming marks. She must have learned early on not to fight back.

April leaves, before returning with a box of supplies. As she hands a shampoo and conditioner to August, I finally get a chance to look at her properly. She's the opposite of August, and for a moment I wonder if they're biologically siblings. Her dark hair is swept up neatly into a chignon, and her sharp eyes are dark brown, almost black and framed with thick dark lashes. Her mouth is full, almost pouty and when it pulls into a cruel smile my heart stops. Dressed all in black and with a small frame, she looks like some sort of fantasy assassin or deadly double agent.

"The best behaved, as always Lilac," she praises as she hands me a bottle of body wash with a flannel. Reading the label, I almost drop it. "Lilac for our Lilac."

I rub my thumb over the tab. *Lilac Oakridge. August*

5th, *2000. O negative.* I hadn't gone by that name since I was sixteen. I'd changed my name legally at eighteen to Lila Johnson and moved away from the small town I'd grown up in, desperate to leave behind the pitying looks and nasty whispers that followed me. I wasn't Lilac. I wasn't that scared little girl anymore.

"No." The word slips from my mouth before I can stop it.

April arches her brow, "No?"

Everyone pauses, even Rose stops fighting against her handler. Six pairs of eyes burn into me, waiting to see what I'll do.

"No. My name is Lila Johnson." I don't understand why I say it, why this is the thing that triggers me but I can't let it go unchallenged. I am not Lilac. Not anymore. "Lilac Oakridge is dead."

She died the night I turned eighteen, and I walked away from every person who'd played a hand in 'raising' me. Every person who pushed me down, who made me cry, who forced me to beg. Everyone who'd left bruises or taken what I wasn't willing to give. Lilac vanished with them.

"Cute." April laughs, before backhanding me so hard I crumple to my knees, not expecting the blow. "Don't talk back to me and learn your place *Lilac.*"

I cup my burning cheek and move my fingers over

my lip. Feeling sticky wetness there, I held back my anger, I'd cut my lip with my teeth when she'd hit me.

No one moves and the silence is heavy with fear and anticipation. Were they expecting an outburst from me? Tears? Begging? I wouldn't give them the satisfaction.

"What are you gawping at? Get them washed!" April barks, before heading back towards the doorway leaving her minions to help Rose and Poppy clean up.

August follows her, and I don't miss the way he grabs her arm, his grip biting into her skin until she shoves him away with a glare. Her words are hissed and low, but I still manage to hear them over the water. "Don't be weak, Auggie."

August

I don't understand why April hit her. Something had obviously rattled Lilac when she'd read the label of her soap, but hadn't she been so well-behaved? Didn't that earn her a small degree of leniency? Was it wrong to show empathy? Compassion? I didn't know anymore. I did what my father asked of me, what April said I must but that didn't mean I was happy to work in the gardens.

I'd stormed after April, grabbing her arm, trying to understand her thinking. Lilac was no threat. Even if she escaped this room, where would she go? The surrounding acres were ours, there was nothing out there but trees, vines and poisonous plants.

"Don't be weak, Auggie" my sister growls as we stand facing off in the doorway, her dark eyes burning into mine. We were always on the same side, a team, but this didn't sit right with me. Pushing away my hand, she leaves the room.

I inhale slowly, exhaling after the count of five. I trusted April, she was my sister. The only one who'd ever stood up for me, the one who'd protected me from Father's wrath when we were children and even now as adults.

We were products of one of his first harvests, but where April was accepted despite her fertility issues, I was a failure. I was a weed that should have been eradicated at birth, but for some unknown reason my father had a soft spot for my mother and when she'd helped nourish his flowerbed, he couldn't dispose of me. Is that love? When you can't turn your progeny into mulch? Or is it foolish sentimentality that held him back from achieving greatness with his harvest?

I return to Lilac, who's still on her knees on the cold tile, water streaming down her body and I'm ashamed of the urge to touch her that rises up. I want to pull her to my chest and hold her, keep her safe like April kept me.

But that's weak, just like April said. I can't get attached to the flowers. I am not a horticulturist like Father, I can't risk ruining his sowing or germinating processes. And I want to. I want to grab Lilac, take her to my room and shut out everyone else.

I can still feel the warmth from her touch earlier. As hemophiliac bruises were nothing new to me, but something inside me was restless at seeing her ankle mottled with purple and black. I'd wanted to help, to ease some of her pain, but her hands on mine had been a hard reminder that I wasn't worthy of a flower like Lilac.

My father often brought in his friends, other horticulturists and florists to help with germinating his crop. Their donations are what kept The Arboretum running, since the house itself was expensive to maintain, without taking into consideration the Greenhouse or the gardens. The blooms he sold were worth a fortune, the last sprout sold for $30,000 since the mother had been a natural redhead and that seemed to increase the price tag. Dahlia. That had been her name, and now Father was growing the most beautiful red dahlias in his greenhouse. The Harvest from them would bring yet more money to keep the gardens going.

I don't know what it was about Father's death blooms that people loved, but he never had to dispose of stock as other florists might. His order book was always full, and a waiting list ensured that no flower went to waste. He saw himself as a creator of life, in so many ways and he was right. He created life twice over with each process, with the sprouts during The Harvest and again with The Second Harvest before recycling the remains and starting the process again.

Lilac struggles to wash her hair with her hands cuffed together, so I step forward and begin working the shampoo into a lather in her dark curls. She freezes for a moment, before relaxing and letting me help.

"Thank you," she says quietly, staring at the tiles straight ahead. "For being kind to me."

She is tiny compared to me, her head coming to my shoulder and as we stood inches apart, I knew her small frame would slot easily into mine should I choose to close the gap between us. The sweet, heady scent of lilacs fills my nose as she pours the body wash on a flannel and begins soaping her arms as I clean her hair. It's all oddly comfortable and domestic in a way I didn't think I'd ever experience. I was flawed. A failed strain. I didn't get to have this.

Shaking away that thought, I remove my fingers from her hair and turn her body, so we're facing one another before I tilt her head back under the water. The soap suds swirl down the drain as her violet eyes watch me, a bone-tired weariness in them that I feel all the way down to my toes. Suddenly I felt exhausted like my body was being weighed down by everything and I was on the verge of drowning.

I turn her back and repeat the process with the conditioner and this time when she spins to face me, she continues to soap her body, flannel tracing lazy suds across her stomach and down over her hips, below to between her thighs.

Pushing her head back, her lips part and I want to taste her. To feel her moan beneath my mouth. I know she knows, and I swear it's like she can see into my mind as the small smile she gives me makes my skin feel like it's on fire. I'm a grown man, twenty-seven years old. Twenty-seven-year-olds shouldn't still be blushing every time a pretty woman smiles at them. Except this wasn't any pretty woman, this was Lilac.

The woman I'd watched for weeks.

The woman I'd cultivated.

The woman I'd cared for.

The woman I wanted for myself.

I step back, holding my hands up as if she was

pointing a gun at me and I see the confusion on her sweet features. Opening my mouth, I move to explain, but before anything can leave my lips, April returns.

"Bring them upstairs. Father is ready for them."

———

We guide them into Father's parlor, a large room with a fireplace and ceiling to floor bookshelves. There's a huge leather sofa, with matching armchairs and a beautiful oak coffee table. A dark, brooding bouquet made of Ecuadorian Black orchids, calla lilies, Memory Lane roses and midnight mystic hyacinths dominates the table.

"Get to your knees, and when my father enters do not make eye contact unless he initiates it."

The flowers are all still naked, and I can't help the way my eyes roam over Lilac's curves, her hair slick against her skin as it clings to her back. She gracefully slides down to her knees, palms flat on her thighs and my dick twitches in response. Christ, she was going to be the death of me and I couldn't even touch her.

Rose is the last to move, and it isn't until April uses her foot on the back of her knees that she finally crumples onto the carpet.

Grabbing Rose's wet hair, April yanks it back and

closes the space between them. "You won't need your tongue for germination, so I won't hesitate to rip it out if you disobey me. Understand?"

When Rose nods tightly, April grins and licks a strip up the side of her face. The two nursery workers leave so that it's only me and April waiting with the flowers for Father.

"I think he'll be pleased with these ones. I mean, I know he's always happy with the quality we provide, but I have a good feeling about this crop. I heard he's already had several interested parties for Lilac and Rose. I guess some gardeners like a challenge."

I shoot Lilac a glance, noticing her tense as April mentions her name. The idea of Father's business partners touching her makes me feel like something bitter is uncoiling in the pit of my stomach. I don't understand how she elicits these reactions from me, it's not like she's the first flower I've ever handled. I'd been helping in the nursery with my father since I turned fourteen, but I'd never felt this way towards any of the crops.

My father strides into the room and I take a moment to watch him. His greying hair and mustache make him look like a distinguished gentleman, instead of the creative genius he is.

He's wearing a three-piece suit, with an antique

silver pocket watch tucked neatly into his waistcoat. Today he's using a black cane with a decorated silver handle, even though there's nothing wrong with him, he just thinks it makes him look more refined.

"Children, I am very impressed with the flowers you've provided ready for germination. They're exquisite." He praises us as he walks around them, reaching out and gently running his fingers over their soft skin as if they were petals ready for inspection. Leaning in, he inhales the scent of each delicate flower. The body wash they'd used earlier was created especially for them, using organic materials we grew here at The Arboretum and fragranced according to their own species. Our skincare range was one of our biggest sellers on the normal market, while the sprouts and death blooms were popular at the Mortality Market. I waver, fists clenched as he runs the tip of his cane down Lilac's spine, but to her credit, she doesn't move or pull away and something almost like pride settles over my skin. Good girl.

Finally, he takes a seat on the sofa, pushing out the tails of his jacket before he gets comfortable and I roll my eyes. April catches me and frowns in warning since we both know that he won't hesitate to use that cane on me if he sees my disrespect.

"Our aim here is to produce the best quality sprouts

and blooms. In order to do that we take care of you, we feed and water you, we help you grow. It is easier to do this if you're cooperative since we do hate to deadhead any troublesome flowers." His voice is calm and kind as he talks to the women. He always was a charmer; it's why he'd established himself so easily with his unique venture. "Any questions?"

I watch her throat bob as she swallows, obviously building up the courage to say something. "What do you plan to do with us exactly?"

"Lilac, isn't it? April tells me you're very amiable and I'm pleased to see you're so well-mannered as well as beautiful." My father smiles, it's endearing and undoubtedly fake. Lilac's spine stiffens, ever so slightly and if I wasn't focused on her, I might miss it.

April moves to stand beside me, and I know she's grinning, I can feel the waves of smugness pouring off her. She's pleased with how our father is interacting with them, happy with how docile they're being and excited to move onto the next stages. She's always the same, The Harvest is her end goal and she'll do anything to achieve it.

"First we germinate you, don't worry—we have the best florists and horticulturists from around the world on hand to assist with this."

Lilac frowns but this time it's Poppy who speaks, "Germinate?"

"Yes Poppy, we will help you to produce a sprout, which can then be sold and planted in another garden to be cherished and adored."

What the buyer did with the sprout was none of our business, some raised them as their own, others used them for more depraved pursuits. Once the exchange happened, we were absolved of all responsibility, *caveat emptor* and all that.

"A baby?" Rose hisses, mouth twisted with disgust as Poppy's shoulders begin to shake and big, fat silent tears fall down her cheeks.

April pours my father a glass of whiskey from the side cabinet behind us. Sliding the glass onto the table in front of him, we give the flowers a moment to process.

"We don't call them that dear," my father's voice is condescending as he takes a sip of the amber liquid, swirling the ice around the glass with a clink.

"What happens after that? We just keep producing more...sprouts?" Lilac's face is closed off, her mouth pulled into a tight line and I remember what she said about her body not being her own. Who hurt her? Who broke her so that she no longer cried?

"Heavens no." He chuckles, "To keep our supply fresh, rare and in demand, each flower only germinates once. After that, you'll help the blooms with The Second Harvest."

My stomach clenches, his words reminding me that time was finite. Lilac could easily slip through my fingers and into the soil before I was ready for it. My throat feels tight as I bite back a cough and April shoots me a concerned glance.

"And what does that mean?"

It meant she would become mulch. Feed for The Harvest. It would be painful and drawn out, but the flowers would be unlike anything you'd ever seen. Her suffering would create awe-inducing beauty. There was a delicacy to death blooms that could not be found anywhere else.

Standing once again, my father waves his hand dismissively at them. "That's a conversation for another day."

CHAPTER THREE

Lilac

The sick feeling that settled in my stomach last night refuses to shift, instead it's like I can taste acid every time I swallow or inhale too deeply. We were incubators. They were going to breed us, like cows to grow children that they were then going to sell. I didn't live in a bubble; I knew that human trafficking was a global problem—I'd seen the statistics. I just never imagined that it would look like this...

Instead of taking us back to the cells after our

conversation with 'Father', as he insisted we call him, we were taken upstairs and shown to bedrooms. They were sparsely decorated, but pure luxury compared to what we'd been used to for the past week. A large double bed with fresh, plump bedding dominated the room. A dresser was tucked away near the window alongside a washbasin and a small armchair was positioned in front of an open fireplace that I doubt they'd ever let me light in case I tried to burn the place down.

"If you so much as blink at me wrong, you'll be back in the cell and on reduced rations." April had warned us as she'd led us up the stairs.

None of us responded, because there was nothing to say. August sticks so closely behind me that I swear I can feel his breath dancing over my skin with every other step we take but he's careful not to touch me. After he tenderly washed my hair yesterday, I'm even more sure that he's going to be my ticket out of here, I just need to find a way to dig my fingers in and drag him closer into my web.

April carried on giving us a rundown as she showed us where the bathroom was since we'd be sharing one. "Breakfast is at 7:30 am and afterward you'll be beginning a new exercise program."

"Exercise program?" Poppy questioned as we stood outside the room that was about to become hers.

"Yes, Father wants you all in optimal condition for sowing and germination."

They wanted us in optimal condition.

Optimal condition.

Those two words rattle around in my chest, making everything ache. "And if we aren't?"

April grinned, and I was right. A Cheshire cat grin set my teeth on edge. "We don't encourage weeds to grow, we deadhead them."

I didn't need her to explain what that meant to me, we all understood the threat she was making. Be healthy and fertile and obedient, or become plant food.

She'd reached across and unlocked Poppy's handcuffs, before showing her into the room followed by one of the men from earlier. Standing outside in the corridor we heard her explain that his name was Lars, and he was Poppy's new handler. He's responsible for making sure she's healthy and behaving, and he's allowed to use any discipline he sees fit as long as it does not cause permanent damage.

Rose trembled beside me as April's words fill the space around us, like black tar trying to work its way into our lungs. We went through the same production when we got to the next room and Poppy was shown inside. Her handler was called Jason, but April promised to keep a very close eye on her since she required extra attention.

My room was the last but one down the corridor and April came inside with August and made herself comfortable on my bed, sprawling out on the covers.

"I told you that your good behavior would be rewarded...and as such, August is going to be your handler. He's easy to get along with, quiet and I feel like you guys have already built up a rapport."

"Oh," I'd breathed, glancing sideways at August, who stood beside the fireplace, green eyes locked onto my face like it always was every time I looked up.

She was pleased with herself as she pulled out her phone and began scrolling. After a minute or so she snorts at something, mutters something that sounds like 'Thea's artwork is trippy man' and tucks it back in her pocket before leveling me with a strange glare. "Aren't you going to thank me?"

"Thank you," I mumbled, looking down at my feet. There was something biting in her words, and the hair on my arm stands on end.

I knew what this is, I recognized it. It's the moment right before something switches. It's the flip, the other shoe dropping, the push to go into fight or flight mode. I've been here before and I know I have a fawn response.

I know I'm going to try and placate whatever this is because I can't run. There's nowhere to run.

"Like you mean it Lilac." There it was. I could hear the change as the words dripped with sadism, and I could almost feel the power trip she was about to embark on. Why were all assholes in my life power-hungry, tyrannical despots? First my father, then my foster parents, one after the other and now this.

"Thank you," I straightened my body and raised my eyes to meet hers, forcing a mask of sincerity on my face. I deliberately kept my voice low and soft, hoping that it would be enough to placate her, but she'd sat up on my bed and shuffled towards the end, and I knew it wasn't.

"Hmm, I'm not convinced." Her voice was hard as she'd commanded, "Kneel."

I slid down to the cool carpet, ignoring the way it scratched against my skin. I'd spent more time on my knees yesterday than I had in a long time, and if April thought I'd forget that she was wrong. I'd escape, I'd find my freedom and then I would get my revenge.

Her foot bobbed in front of my face, she was wearing workbooks that had mud embedded in the stitching, and carried the scent of wet grass. "Kiss my boots."

The position forced me to lean forward, and I could feel the cool air shift down my spine. August stepped forward, and I knew that if I shifted a little more, he'd have a full view of my pussy. Was that the best way to reach him? To make him mine? Without hesitating, I'd pushed my legs wider apart and pressed my lips to April's boot. There was something about being the center of attention that had a swirl of lust unfurling in my stomach. I wasn't a fool, I knew it was a physical reaction—nothing more. But I still hated myself for it.

April reached down and grabbed my hair, pulling my head back. "What do you think, Auggie? Does she seem grateful to you?"

Her dark eyes were shining, and I could see how much she was enjoying. She was feeding on the power dynamic, not just with me on my knees at her feet but also in the way she made August watch. April dominates everything around her, everything except her father and that was something I needed to exploit if I had a hope in hell in making this sick family fall apart.

"Lick it. From toe to heel, Lilac. I want it to be so slick with your spit that I can see my own reflection in it." The words had sent another lick of heat through me and I leaned further down until I'm practically face down on the floor with my ass fully in the air, hands propping me in place.

My tongue swiped over the leather of her boot first, and it's soft and glossy in no time with my spit. Using the tip, I look up at April and work my way over the stitching and grooves, swirling my tongue around the eyelets, making sure I paid the detailing lots of attention. The outsole is rough and rubbery under my mouth, and I have to keep swallowing to keep everything wet, but it's worth it because when I look up, her pupils are blown and her mouth has fallen open. Behind me I can hear August's breathing, it's heavier and staggered now as if he can barely control himself and that turns me on even more.

"Hmmm much better, isn't that right Auggie?" April purrs, before withdrawing her boot enough to place it on my shoulder and force me down, cheek crushed against the carpet. "I told you, well-behaved flowers get rewards."

As she stands, I stay in position, partly afraid and partly turned on. A warm hand runs down my spine and over the curve of my ass before delicate fingers brush over my swollen lips. There's no ceremony as she plunges her fingers inside me, unapologetically with no hesitation. I can't help the small gasp that leaves me or the way my hips make a small aborted thrust. Shame floods me and my skin heats, *what the fuck Lila?!*

Her other hand swats my ass cheek before a finger gazes at my asshole and my body clenches. "I think you like this." A strangled moan filled the room and it took a few minutes before I realized the noise came from me.

August moved, and I could see his boots out of the corner of my eye. Still, he says nothing, just stands, silently watching like always.

"You've been well trained," April hummed as she fucked me roughly, using her thumb to brush over my clit harshly. There was no clear rhythm and my body, overwhelmed with the last week and the whole situation didn't seem to know what to do.

When I'd finally come, April laughed and continued forcing her fingers inside me until it's almost unbearable. I was overstimulated and as my eyes began to water, I whimpered. Finally, she pulled away and I sat up slowly watching as she smiled at August. Rubbing her palm over his obvious hard-on, she'd laughed and hooked her fingers through his belt loops before pulling him from the room. Shame made bile rise in my throat, April's hands on my body should have disgusted me. She'd made me come, forced me to my knees and taken control of my traitorous body.

I knew rationally that it stemmed from my trauma, I knew that I had twisted responses to being touched, a chasm between my mind and body that I was barely able to bridge on my good days. Facing my reaction to her would mean unpacking thoughts I wasn't ready to have. So instead, I push it down, ball it up and throw it over my shoulder to be dealt with later. I had no headspace to dissect the only piece of pleasure I'd had since I'd arrived here.

Before April left she reminded me to be ready for breakfast in the morning. That is what I was doing now, pulling on a jumper and a pair of yoga pants ready to be escorted downstairs as I ruminated on what I'd learned yesterday. August was protective over me for some reason and in return, he was April's weakness. Their relationship went beyond siblings, they were twisted up in each other, but how tangled up their roots were had yet to be seen. Their father was a wall between them. I'd seen the eyeroll August had for his progenitor and the way April had hung onto *Father's* every world. Where was their mother? Slowly, the seeds were being planted in my head. All I had to do was grow them before creating a garden of my own.

August

A glance at the alarm clock tells me it's almost time to collect Lilac for breakfast as part of our new routine. Ignoring April's snores beside me, I creep carefully from the bed. We were family. She and I were roots, entwined together, grown together and to pull us apart would ruin the flower bed...it would destroy us both. April was my protector, my friend, my voice when Father silenced me. We were from The First Harvest, and although we were flawed, not suitable for replanting, Father still kept us. April was infertile, which made her unsuitable for harvesting but she was capable of assisting father in ways I was not. It was why he favored her. Why she was his heir. And together we lived in The Arboretum, the only constant in the gardens.

But when I look at Lilac it's like the soil is shifting beneath my feet. She was the thing I craved. She made me want...more. I'd never wanted a flower for myself, not until I'd been standing outside her shitty apartment building, and as I'd watched her go about her dreary life, I knew she was meant for me. It had been three days since she licked April's boot and she's been nothing but obedient and observant since, something that pleased Father. Watching her that night, exposed and raw as she'd moaned through her orgasm had shown me that there was no escaping what I felt for her. I wanted it to be her beside me in the bed, softly snoring and I knew that those traitorous thoughts were dangerous. I can feel guilt and shame creeping into my chest as I pull my clothes on and leave the room, April oblivious to my departure. I couldn't let Father germinate her with his associates. I couldn't watch her grow, heavy and swollen with their sprout. She was mine. Mine to protect, mine to care for.

Knocking softly on her door, my heart clenches at the warm smile she gives me when it swings open. Today her hair is swept back up into a ponytail, and she's wearing a plain black t-shirt and a pair of black shorts.

"Look, we match!" She laughs as gestures at her clothes and then her hand sweeps over me, in my own all-black outfit. Her hand hovers over my body, never touching and yet I feel myself lean into it, desperate to close the gap. "We look like we're in a gang or maybe partners in crime."

My breathing stutters and I almost trip over my own feet as she winks, violet eyes twinkling. I wanted every morning to start like this, with her teasing and smiling just for me. Failures like me didn't get flowers. I wasn't allowed to have her, and so if this was all I could get then I'd enjoy these snatched moments between us.

I expected her to have questions about April, but she says nothing and I find myself grateful but also disappointed. If she was interested in me, surely she would care? However, I also had no words to describe what April and I were to one another. It was complicated.

The sound of Lilac's laughter must have woken the others, as Poppy steps into the corridor, face pale, with dark circles under her eyes.

A second later, my door cracks open and April slips out wearing yesterday's clothes. When she sees Lilac and me, her face splits into a grin and there it is again, that guilty gnawing as Lilac tenses. "Auggie! Can you take them down to breakfast and then get them started on the yoga?"

I nod as Rose and the other handlers appear too, like some sort of weird congress in the corridor.

"Yoga?" Lilac questions softly avoiding looking at April and instead glances across to the others.

Yesterday father had them swimming laps naked in the pool after breakfast before some sort of weights training in the afternoon. He was serious about their health, that's why his flowers were worth so much money, plus it keeps them tired and achy, which dampens the resistance.

April shrugs, and I notice she's holding one of my jumpers which she pulls on without hesitation. "It will help with germinating and also with the growth of the sprout."

Glancing back to Lilac, she's no longer looking at

me, her eyes on the other two. Her body seems stiff, the lines from her smile gone. Maybe she was jealous? The thought makes me perk up a little, as I ignore the voice telling me that it's not possible, I am a failure. An imperfect creation.

"What about...delivery?" Rose asks, choking out the words.

With a huge stretch before using the back of her hand to cover a wide yawn, April sounds bored as she sighs, "Father doesn't believe that labor is necessary for the process. You'll be harvested when the time is right."

It's so quiet you could hear a pin drop, even though the whole hallway is carpeted. It's like we're standing in a bubble, with the air being slowly sucked out. Out of the corner of my eye, I see Lilac's throat bob as she swallows back whatever it is she's feeling.

"Harvested?" Poppy squeaks, finally breaking the silence, while Rose hisses.

Ignoring the flowers and the panic that appears to be blossoming between them, April grabs my arm and gives it a squeeze. "Auggie...get Mrs. Danvers to send up some coffee? I think I overdid it last night."

Bowing my head, I motion for Lars and Jason to begin herding them downstairs before something happens. I can feel it, like water rising just before a flood and if I don't move them away from April, she'll say something that disrupts the very fine balance with which we were currently maintaining.

"April, what does harvesting mean?" Her mouth is pulled into a tight line, almost like she's chewing the insides of her cheeks as Lilac places her hand over April's on my arm. The move is territorial somehow like she wants to peel April away from me, and to my amazement it works as April drops her hand, moving away from both of us.

"Lilac, Jesus. Just stop with the questions okay." The look she gives is a warning, April may have favorites, but they were just flowers at the end of the day. Easily replaceable and nothing more than a means to an end.

———

"April, you truly did a fine job with this lot." My father muses as he takes a sip of his sweet tea. "That fucker Gray has nothing on me when it comes to producing quality."

His obsession with the other artists on the Mortality Market was going to be his downfall one day. My father is currently sitting on the back porch, next to my sister watching the new crop do their yoga, all shaky legs and stretched arms in the sunshine. It would almost be peaceful if it wasn't for the extra handlers surrounding them.

The Greenhouse shimmers in the light just behind them, dominating the view, while the vineyards and trees enclose the back lawn. My father truly has built his own little world here, and as he continues to discuss future plans with April, practically ignoring my presence, I wonder how long I'll be allowed to remain a part of it.

Lilac moves through the poses Celeste is showing them with ease, her body shifting gracefully like she'd done this before even though I hadn't seen her near a yoga studio in the two weeks I'd cultivated her.

Celeste is yet another of my father's associates. It was amazing what money and power could do for a person, the influence they had. It meant no one ever looked twice, or too closely at the kingdom my father created and in return he filled the world with his beauty. It was the same for the staff on-site at The Arboretum, they were all paid handsomely or depraved enough to want to be here just so they could bask in his genius, hoping for some scraps. Loyalty had a price tag in our world, and my father could afford to pay it twice over.

There's a sudden shout and a burst of movement disrupts the calm of the morning. April rolls her eyes as she watches Rose dart between two handlers trying as she tries to make a run for the trees. If only she knew what was waiting for her out there, then she wouldn't be so keen to hide amongst the plants. Rose's scream is cut off as Lars tackles her to the ground with a heavy thud and I see Lilac flinch at the impact.

She's dragged towards the porch steps, thrashing and flailing around like a fish caught out of water. She even manages to throw her head back and catch Lars, bloodying his nose before he backhands her and forces her to her knees.

"Disobedience won't be tolerated here, Rose." He talks to her like she's a small child who's been caught with her hand in the cookie jar, rather than a flower who's trying to escape. There's a subdued sigh before my father takes another sip of his tea. "Jason, you know the drill."

Jason is her handler. He was the one trusted to educate her, and her behavior is a reflection on him and now he's the one to punish her. This little hierarchy is yet another way my father keeps his minions in line, and part of his power structure. They want to work their way up, they want to do well for him. April once laughed about the handlers having praise kinks, but a part of me wonders if that isn't the truth.

"Yes, sir." Everyone stops to watch as Jason

unsheathes a knife from his belt and strides towards Rose with determination.

Lars keeps her down on her knees, his hands on her shoulders pinning her in place as she squirms and cries. Gripping her chin, he tilts her face upwards for Jason, who forces his fingers into her mouth and grabs her tongue. Keeping it held firmly between his thumb and forefinger, he pulls it out as far as he can, making Rose gag.

"I warned you Rose, but still you tried to run." Jason's words hold a similar tone to my father's, and I know he's made another man a monster in his image. Aster Bramwell was the ultimate creator after all, a god in his own mind.

My father stands, and using his pompous cane, moves the edge of the porch to get a better view. "A tongue isn't essential to your purpose here. Removal of it will be a painful reminder of your insubordination."

Jason slices through the muscle with little difficulty, blood gushing from the pulpy mess left behind, pouring out of Rose's mouth and flowing freely down her neck, between her breasts and onto the grass, feeding the soil.

Her keening howls aren't anything we haven't heard before, she isn't the first to take the inch my father gives and try to claim a mile. When I was younger, I used to hate the ones who ran—I thought they were ungrateful.

My father doted on them, gave them everything before he turned their bodies into art. Now I understand better.

April motions for our father to sit before casting her eye over the rebellious rose. "Take her to her room. Do not provide her with any pain relief, she needs to be reminded of her role here and her place in the process."

She wasn't the only one who needed to be reminded. Every day I spent near Lilac was another where I questioned my father's methods. What if it had been her? Could I stand idly behind April and my father as she was mutilated? No, I would be the one forced to cut her, to cause her pain. My hands tremble at the thought. She would be crushed in my careless hands before she could bloom if I didn't act soon.

CHAPTER FOUR

Lilac

They cut her tongue out. Like, just sliced it right out of her head and I was expected to go back to practicing some shitty weird lotus position afterward as though nothing had happened. Tears stream down Poppy's face and as we carry on with Celeste, I can hear her muted sobs surround me, a stark reminder that I was playing a very deadly game. It was clear that Father had more money and influence than I could have imagined, I mean we were doing yoga in his garden for fuck's sake and no one batted an eyelid. There was a dark patch, where Rose's blood had stained the grass and Celeste hadn't done anything other than appearing extremely irritated that we'd disrupted her stretching session.

Inhaling, I focus and re-center myself. When I was six, my foster father at the time, Kevin, had locked me in the basement for two days with only a bowl of dog food and a bottle of water. It was to teach me 'respect' since I hadn't 'learned' my place because I told the social worker how his son had stolen the chocolate she'd brought with her on her last visit. When I was eight, he'd left me locked out, in the garden in November, to make me 'appreciate' what I had and how he cared for me. When I was nine my second foster father, Cody, had cut all my hair off and told the school it was because I had lice. It wasn't. It was because I needed to know that I was nothing. The third one, Mike, has been the worst. He looked at me like I wasn't a child, and treated me like I was his personal bedwarmer and punching bag. I'd learned back then to take all the pain, hurt and anger and pack it away in a little pouch. Then inside my head, I'd store that pouch in a box, on a shelf at the very back of my mind. It was the only way I could get through every challenge, every new torment and this was no different. I ignore the way my blood thrums in my ears.

It's like an out-of-body experience once again as I close it all out, push away the sounds of Rose howling and Poppy's tears.

Before lunch, we have a little free time and I ask August to walk outside with me, pretending it's so I can bask in the sunlight for a little longer. He gobbles up my lie, and we stroll away from the nightmare mansion and April's watchful glare. His father vanished almost an hour ago to discuss important matters with a business partner from England and Poppy's on the verge of a breakdown, so Lars takes her inside for a nap.

"Will you show me the greenhouse?" I ask as we walk along the tree line, nearing the huge Victorian-style structure. If I could learn a little more about the layout of the grounds, maybe glean some information on where the fuck we even were, then I'd stand a better chance of planning an escape.

August gives me another one of his silent nods, and not for the first time I wonder if he can even speak. He always wears jumpers or hoodies, so I only have a partial view of his neck but nothing seems out of the ordinary. Why doesn't he ever say anything? April seems to talk for him a lot at the house but when it's just us, there should be a way to draw him out of his shell.

Holding the door open for me, I'm conscious of the way August leans in to inhale as I pass. For some reason likes me and I don't think he realizes that he's making it obvious. His hand circles my wrist softly as he leads me towards some vegetable patches to the left of the building. I would be a fool not to explore his attraction, he was my only hope of survival right now and I needed him to be consumed by me. I wanted to occupy his every thought.

I shrug my arm free, smiling at the look of alarm on his face as he tries to anticipate my next move. The confusion and blush that heats his cheeks when I slide my hand into his and interlock our fingers almost make me feel guilty for what I was doing, but in this game, there were no winners or losers, only survivors.

"August, why don't you ever talk?" My voice is quiet like he likes it and I make it as sweet as I can.

Looking away, he swallows, before making a small, awkward coughing noise. I try to ignore his discomfort, pretend that I don't see it as I lean over and inhale the tomato plants. The sweet almost grassy scent reminds me of my grandfather, he used to grow them out on his porch in little ceramic clay pots my grandmother had painted. They were the sum of my good memories, my grandparents. When they died, it was like the last light in my life, small flicker as it was, went out. My father hadn't cared to keep up the pretense of doting father after that, and then I went into the care system.

I feel August's warmth surround me as he leans in with me, eager to keep me close. What was it like to be important to someone? To be their whole world? Did it feel warm like this? Or was it something more suffocating?

"H-h-hurts." August eventually croaks, the word is raspy and rough against my shoulder.

He wasn't silent because he had nothing to say, he was silent because it hurt to be heard. With April leading him around by his nose and his father dictating his life, August shied away from the pain of having to open his mouth and make his own choices. That's why he was nervous with me because I was in the submissive role, the more passive one rather than him for a change.

"Ohh, I'm sorry. Please, shhhh," My pacifying traits creep forward and a small part of me hates myself right now. Why am I placating my captor? Seeing his face wince in pain made me want to shield him, a completely irrational urge.

Lifting our entwined hands, he separates us, to place my fingers over his neck. The skin beneath my touch feels rigid and raised with almost a rubbery texture. They're some sort of burns, maybe chemical, but possibly old since they feel harder than I'd expect if they were fresh. He relaxes into my touch, almost sighing and that's when it dawns on me that this is the way to root myself into his heart.

"Shhhhhh," I soothe, using my free hand to stroke his hair. "Don't waste your words, they're precious. You should save them for the important things."

His eyes light up, and a tendril of guilt creeps in.

"Come on, I want to carry on with our tour. I'm not ready to go back to the house yet." I left the implication that I was not ready to be separated from him hanging heavy in the air between us.

He captures my hand again, giving me a reassuring squeeze as we weave between the vegetable patches before strolling over to the flower beds. The sun streams in through all the huge glass panes, refracting light, casting rainbows over the leafy greens and lush wet soil. Sweat begins to form, my skin is sticky but not in an unbearable way. In another time, another situation, I would have found this almost romantic. The heady sweet smell of all the foliage and vegetation was soothing, and August was gentle with me. Almost reverent as he places a soft kiss on the palm of my hand.

Near the rear of the building, there are large tarpaulin screens erected, obscuring a third of the greenhouse. I begin to guide us towards them, noticing small beeping noises as we move closer. The smell surrounding us becomes thicker, cloying almost as we draw nearer. August stops abruptly, looking at the tarpaulin sheets, face tight, mouth clamped shut as he tugs on my hand, pulling me in the opposite direction.

As carefully as I can, I try to shrug him off and keep walking towards the sheets. "I want to see, just a quick look."

Groaning, he grabs my wrist and tugs me harder. Why was he acting like this? What were they hiding?

The gravel shifts beneath my feet as I try to gain some traction. There was something here, and it was almost in reach.

"What's down there?" I finally tug completely free and take three steps forward. Between the gap in the tarpaulin, I think I can make out machinery, and bamboo canes, wrapped in wires.

"N-o. NO!" He screams, except his voice breaks and instead of sounding forceful, it sounds anguished. It does the trick though, and I stop exactly where I am. His face is flushed, eyes begging me not to take another step.

"It's okay August, I'm not going any closer." Pushing away my disappointment, I resolved to find a way back here later but first I had to appease the hulking, silent man who was my ticket out.

Gingerly, I wrap my arms around his waist, rubbing firm circles into his back as he leans down and presses his lips against my hair. "Lila..."

He struggles to make the 'c' sound with his throat. I know it's not deliberate, but for a moment...for a tiny flash of time, a sandy grain of a second, I'm Lila Johnson again. And I'm here with a man who watches me like I hung the moon, and not a psychopath who kidnapped me for his father to breed like some prized heifer at the farmer's market.

"I hear you," I whisper into his chest, and the tension slowly seeps out of him. He smells like the air after a heavy downpour of rain, fresh and light.

The ringing of his phone, and April's voice calling us for lunch squash the moment, and in the blink of an eye it vanishes as quickly as it came.

"It's time to go, isn't it?" I sound sad, and it takes me a heartbeat or two before I understand that I genuinely am sad. Returning to the house means that I'm just one step closer to spreading my legs for strangers, one step closer to being 'harvested' and I'm still in the dark about what that means.

August pushes me off his chest and looks at me with an expression I can't read. He brushes his thumb over my cheekbone before he places a kiss on my forehead and once his lips leave my skin it's like a shutter has come down as he guides me out of the greenhouse and back to the others.

"You two look...cozy," April teases with that smug

grin of hers as we approach the porch. A flash of teeth just makes her look that much crueler as she crosses her arms and leans against the column. "It's a shame August is a failure, otherwise maybe you could have been his."

What was she talking about? A failure? "I don't understand..."

Leaning forward with a hushed voice, as if she was sharing vital information she chuckles. "August's condition is genetic, so he's not allowed to taint the flower beds."

"His throat?" I frown and look over my shoulder at him. His face is blank, but I don't miss the way the corner of his mouth is pulled down and the faint bloom of pink on his cheeks. Why was she humiliating him? By putting him in his place, she was only making him an easier target for me. I planned to use him. I did. So why did I also have to bunch my fists to stop myself from saying something when she accused him of being a failure? She was supposed to be his family.

Flicking her hair over her shoulder she looks bored. "Oh no, that was a punishment for defying Father. I'm talking about his blood disorder. He's a hemophiliac, and useless to the cycle since a rotten sprout is worth nothing."

My mind reverses and trips back over her words. I store the blood disorder information away for safekeeping and focus on the rest of what she said. Their father had punished August, by taking away his voice. They had silenced his disobedience, and that was something I could use to my advantage. My chest aches for him, as his green eyes meet mine, I know he believes her words. Failure. Useless. Rotten. He was going to 'taint' their little enterprise. My fingers brush against his, barely even a touch but I hoped it conveyed everything I wanted to say. I would be his voice, I would hold him tightly and soothe his broken soul. I would protect him from this awful family filled with crazy people, and in return...he would bleed for me.

August

I know that look, that angry gleam in April's eye as Lilac reaches out and connects us for a brief moment. She'll take chunks out of me tonight for it, make me pay for being weak before forcing me to prove my loyalty. It's what she always does, and yet I can't bring myself to pull away from Lilac.

"I don't think he's useless. He takes care of us,"

Lilac's voice is like honey, coating me in a warmth that makes me smile. April catches my eye and glares, her lip curling in disgust. She liked to play with the crop, but only when she was the one pulling all the strings.

"It's time for lunch unless feasting upon the sight of my brother is enough to fill your stomach?" She scoffs, "No, I didn't think so."

Turning on her heel, she marches off into the house and we follow behind quietly. Poppy is with Lars, about to enter the dining room when April grabs my arm and pulls me away.

"I don't know what's going on, but don't forget your place brother. We are your family. Family comes first." Her words hiss in my ears the way water sounds when it hits the bottom of a hot pan, scorching and lethal.

I shrug myself free of her grasp and take my seat at the table, on the left side of my father. He barely glances at me as I take my seat, and flashes April a large toothy grin when she takes hers. I guess that means he's had a good day down in The Greenhouse today with his little laboratory and his new species.

The staff brings out lunch, which is a cold soup made with the vegetables grown here and fresh crusty bread. Poppy and Lilac begin to eat without ever looking up from their plates and I wish for just a moment that my father and

April weren't here, because then Lilac would smile at me. She would talk to me. It would fill the room, the melody of her voice, and I'm sure it would even make Poppy and Lars smile. Lilac was like that, the light in the bleakness.

My father looks smug as he rips off some bread and thrusts it into his bowl with excited aggression. "The earlier crop is growing well, we should be able to harvest soon.".

"So did the introduction of the sugar water help?" April leans in, and they look so alike in their enthusiasm, their intensity carved into every line on their faces. Her nose is the same as his, as is the shape of her mouth. Her dark coloring on the other hand must come from her flower since our father has hair that's more like mine.

Chuckling, my father has a twinkle in his eye. "Surprisingly yes, we've also added some streptomycin to ensure the flowers survive for longer this time around."

"That's good, and did it slow the germination down significantly?" This was why she was his favorite, despite her inability to produce sprouts. She cared the same way he did, whereas I was here because I had no one else. Father raised me, even though I was a burden when he could have turned me into mulch. Family comes first. But some family members come before others, there's still a hierarchy in love it seems.

His voice changes ever so slightly, an indicator that he's beginning to retreat into his own head to work on the issue. "A little, but we'll see if it's worth it when they bloom. We've also tweaked the amounts in each flower bed to see which ones will yield the best results."

April claps her hands together, making Poppy flinch. "How exciting!"

"Isn't it? To think, we've been doing this here at The Arboretum for over twenty-five years and we're still finding new ways to produce the best bouquets."

"You should be proud, Father." April gushes and it's like a dull ache in the back of my head. He was proud of her, of his plants and his empire. I was never worth more than a backward glance and sitting at this table, I'm reminded of that as another meal passes where he's barely acknowledged my presence.

"The other gardeners will be here in three days," April remarks, twisted in my sheets as she lights up a cigarette. She only smokes when something was bothering her, and never in her room since she hated the way the smell lingered, clinging to all the fabrics.

Standing in front of my mirror, I twist to get a better look at the claw marks she's left on my body. Bloody scratches cover my back and arms, most still oozing thanks to my hemophilia, and teeth marks can be made out on my neck and shoulders. Bruises are scattered over my skin with hickeys, and it's impossible to differentiate between the two as my body is adorned with blooming purple, red and black splodges. I've always bruised easily, and sometimes it feels like April is trying to make art using my skin as her canvas. I knew she would make me pay for earlier, I just wish I didn't have to wear the evidence of her wrath for the next week.

"I can't wait to see Lilac, with tears streaming down her face, absolutely wrecked by Loren Amata." She leans back in the sheet, groaning. "Urghhhhh, the Italian can fuck like a pro."

I raise a brow, catching her gaze in the mirror's reflection. Lilac was being assigned Loren? He was one of father's European investors who wasn't a proper connoisseur of florals, but rather the owner of a vineyard and from a powerful family. He was handsome, young and loved sex with the flowers, it's why he invested so heavily. I suspect he has some kind of breeding kink and this way he never deals with the fallout since the sprouts are sold off. A flash of jealousy shoots through me, what if Lilac liked him better than me? He would be able to talk to her, to touch her body, to kiss her. I wasn't allowed any of those things. She wasn't meant for me...but she was mine. I knew that. I could feel it in my bones. I bite on my tongue until I taste coppery bitterness. What's a little more blood spilled this evening?

April's eyes narrow as she takes in my expressions and I hate how well she's always been able to read me. "I don't understand why you care, Auggie. She's just a shrub, a plaything for father and once she's given him what he wants she'll be recycled like the others."

Recycled. Used for The Second Harvest. I inhale slowly as I feel an unfamiliar emotion rising up my throat, count to ten and exhale. I had time. First, she had to be germinated, then once she was fertilized there were nine months until The First Harvest. That was plenty of time...to what? What is going to change between now and then? I clench my fists, the smell from April's cigarette making me feel nauseous. I knew what would happen, I would become even more attached. It would hurt even more when she was recycled.

"It's me and you brother, always has been, always will be."

Sitting back on the edge of the bed, I ignore April's attempt at reminding me once again of my loyalties. I knew I was playing with fire. I'd know it the first time I'd seen those amethyst eyes.

Stubbing out her disgusting smoke, April crawls towards me until I can feel the warmth radiating off her. An arm wraps around my neck, fingers trailing lazily down my cheek.

"How about this, when Father selects the next crop, we can choose one for you too. Not to germinate of course, but when you're done with her, she can be turned into bone meal. That way it's not a complete waste and you still get to have your fun."

Her words feel like rocks in my stomach. April didn't understand. How could she? She was too much like Father to become attached. Lilac was special, she wasn't just a flower who bloomed once and faded. She was a perennial; she would become more beautiful with every passing spring and to cut that short was wrong. It was cruel.

April must see something because her hand comes around my throat. Biting my earlobe, she moans before reminding me, "She is not yours August, no matter what you think."

The next few days pass very much in the same way. I stand guard over Lilac during the day, dutifully escorting her to the dining room, overseeing her exercise and taking long walks around the vineyard and The Greenhouse with her. We avoid The Nursery, since she isn't ready to see that yet, and to be honest I'm not ready to show her. When she gets a glimpse of the current crop being prepared for The Harvest, she'll finally understand what awaits and I'm not prepared for how she'll react. She's a practical person, logical, she understands that things have to happen the way they do...but when sprouts are introduced into the equation, it changes everything. Seeing the flowers, broken open, ready to become planters for the death blooms is something that cannot be unseen. So, for as long as possible, I'll keep her away from Father and his experimentation process.

My nights are April's. And my body pays the price for it as I leave my room every morning with fresh marks and an ache I can't seem to shake. There's a distance between us that wasn't there before and with every light touch from Lilac, it grows deeper.

Guilt seems to be my constant companion as I knock on Lilac's door, and return her smiles every day. She never asks me about what April and I have, what we are to one another and I'm grateful. It must be obvious with April marking her territory so blatantly but it's another thing that cannot be explained, not without changing how she would look at me. And I need her smiles. Her gentle touches. Her soft words. I need them like I need air to breathe. Lilac is my sun, and like Icarus, I know the fall will be worth the feel of her heat on my skin.

Today is the day that the florists begin to arrive and everyone is on edge as the house is prepared for our guests. The flowers don't know what's happening because Father doesn't believe in tormenting them beforehand, they just know that there are more people in the hallways and bustling around than usual. The theory is that gestation is likely to be more successful if the flowers are relaxed and cared for, they are of course, his perfect vessels. Later at dinner, they'll be given something to help them unwind and even enjoy themselves providing they don't fight it. That's how he's always done it, and it's worked in the past so why bother to change it. My harvest happened this way, so did April's. This was what The Arboretum was created for, to create art in an innovative, genius way. It's why Father's death blooms were world-renowned. So why did it all suddenly feel so fucking wrong?

CHAPTER FIVE

Lilac

Something was wrong. The last two weeks had been no picnic, from the second I'd been kidnapped and woke up in a shitty cell to April trying to get under my skin my hurting August daily. This was different...there was a palpable energy in the house, the tension in the air thrumming with electricity as rooms were aired out and cleaned. Was Father expecting guests? Was it time for the germination or whatever the fuck they called it?

Being here was messing with my head more as each day passed. On one hand, I was here against my will, plucked from my life and put in a vase of some stranger's home. They were going to breed me. Breed me. Every time I think about it, a wave of sickness hits me. Even outside the foster system, I was still nothing more than a body, a combination of parts that rarely functioned as a whole. On the other hand, I was healthy, well-fed, and for want of a better word...cared for. August doted on me, following me everywhere, finding any excuse just to brush against me and the way he looked at me could set the world on fire with its intensity. Was this how they did it? Did they want us to feel secure before they tortured and killed us? Did they get off on fucking with us psychologically as well as using us as baby carriers? It hurt my head dwelling on it for too long, especially since I couldn't do anything about it. At least, not yet. I had a feeling that the answers I needed were in The Greenhouse and The Nursery since those were the two areas August tried to steer me away from the most.

I was trying to formulate a plan to get myself in there when April comes into the dining room and tells us it's time for a shower. We showered daily, so this wasn't strange but it was usually after the exercise sessions and not after breakfast. The grin she flashes me sets my teeth on edge and the predatory look on her face tells me that whatever is happening is not going to be pleasant for us. April, I'd come to learn, thrived off pain. She wanted Rose to fight against her. Wanted August to covet me. That way she had a reason to punish them, she was like my foster father in that respect.

Lars, Jason and August escort us to the wet room that I'd kind of grown used to by now. We strip and leave our clothes in a pile to be washed. Handing us our usual soaps, and lotions, April also hands us a razor.

"Shave everything. And if you don't, I will," Her glare is directed at Rose, who barely even looks up anymore. Since they'd cut out her tongue, she'd sunk further into herself, her defiant streak wiped clean away as if it had been written in sand. "And I don't have the steadiest hands."

Leaning against the back wall, April looks almost bored as she scrolls through her phone. "If they try anything, snap their necks. We don't have time for drama this weekend."

I swear I hear her mumbling to herself, something along the lines of, 'Huh, I didn't realize you could do that with resin' before she pockets the device and steps towards me.

Poppy hesitates, whimpering as Lars turns on her water. After a few moments where they stand locked in staring competition, Poppy concedes and steps under the warm water.

"What's going on?" she asks as she begins to wash her hair.

"We're just preparing you. This weekend we'll begin the germination process. Isn't that exciting?" April grins again. One day I was going to wipe that smug smile off her face, preferably with my first or maybe even a knife. I could go all Joker on her ass.

August stands to the side of me, fingers brushing against mine as he avoids looking at my naked body. It's cute, his crush on me and the way he's trying to show me that he's respectful, even if he is the monster who kidnapped me and brought me here.

Moving behind me, April trails her fingers over my skin, her nails scratching lightly, making my flesh pebble.

"Don't worry Lilac, we've paired you with someone special. Loren likes it rough and hard, all night long…" Her hand wraps around my waist and slides down to rest below my belly button. She laughs into my neck before nipping my earlobe. "Chill Auggie, I'm just letting her know what to expect tonight."

August grabs my wrists and stands before me now, his eyes darting between me and his sister with a weariness that makes me feel almost safe. His thumb traces a reassuring circle on the inside of my wrist, he wants me to know that he won't let her hurt me. His green eyes harden when they flick back to April, and I feel her flinch, ever so slightly.

Her hand dips lower until she's cupping my pussy. "I'm sure it's you she'll be thinking of as Loren makes her come. And as his spunk trickles down her leg, she can lay there and understand that you will never be hers."

April sinks her teeth into my neck so hard it makes my knees buckle and I feel it when she breaks the skin. She's holding me up with one hand on my neck, the other between my legs but slowly we slide to the floor. Grabbing her hair, August pulls her mouth off me, careful not to yank too hard since she seems to resist him.

Once I'm free, he pushes her back onto the tiled floor, where she cackles, mouth glistening with ruby smears. "You can't have her, August. Stop living in a dream world."

August snarls and the sound makes my stomach clench. I never thought someone being territorial over me would be a turn-on, since I'd never felt like my body was my own, but this was different. She hurt me, and that made him furious. Clutching my neck, I ignore the throbbing and make sure she hasn't actually bitten a chunk out of me. When I'm sure the wounds are superficial, I get to my feet and glare down at her, saying nothing. I don't need to. August had made all the noise we needed to.

With a scoff, she gets up and her cocky attitude is back in place as she practically sings excitedly, "Wash up flowers, because tonight you might bloom!"

Handing me the lilac body wash, August's face is full of concerned lines, his forehead furrowed and his mouth drawn into a tight line. I let my hand fall away and show him that I'm not hurt, not really. His hand wraps around my nape and brushes his thumb tenderly over the indents of April's teeth.

"I'm okay. It barely even stings," I reassure him as I get on with washing my hair and shaving every inch of my body as if my life depended on it. Not because she told me to, but because he was watching and I wanted his eyes glued to me. He was going to know every curve, every dimple and freckle on my body by the time I finished if he didn't already. The cracks were beginning to appear in his relationship with April, and I was going to be the stubborn dandelion, growing between them, making the rift bigger until the ground was compromised. It was a case of surviving. Thriving. And I refused to let them pull me from the soil and harvest me, whatever the heck that was.

D inner that evening is the same as always, except Father doesn't join us. He has guests visiting in a second dining room, and we can hear their laughter and chatter down the hall.

Rose sits with her face blank, eyes dead as she picks at her food like a baby bird. Poppy is the one crying this time, her stoic facade crumbling under the weight of the reality of this sick human trafficking game Father was playing. Lars leans in and whispers something in her ear and her shoulders sink, and not for the first time I wonder about their dynamic.

This evening, as it's a special occasion we're served wine with the meal and even though I'd never been a big drinker, I gulp back the almost purple-colored liquid, barely savoring the rich flavor and gagging on the bitter aftertaste.

I hold my glass out for a refill, but August places his hand on my arm and guides it back to the table. His eyes flash with something I don't understand and it isn't until my limbs begin to feel heavy that it hits me. The wine wasn't a treat, it was a trick.

My body feels wrong like I need to crawl out of my skin or I'll burst at the seams. Looking around the table, I see the panic on Poppy's face as she squirms against

Lars, as Rose grunts and groans with tears streaming down her face, and I know they're just as frightened as I am. Scared, but also on fire. I feel as though if August doesn't touch me in the next ten minutes I'll combust.

Stroking my hair, he scoops me up out of my chair and carries me to my room, where the bedding has been changed and the lights are turned down low. I nuzzle my face against his neck as I shift my body, needing friction, needing a connection of some sort. Placing me gently on the bed, I reach out and grab his hair before he can pull away, bringing his mouth against mine in a sloppy, desperate kiss. My mind swirls, my body not feeling like my own and in this moment all I know is that I need him. His hands, his mouth, whatever I can get, I just need him. Wrapping one of my legs around his hip, I grind against him, feeling his erection pressed against me. I'm trying to deepen our kiss when there's a sharp knock at the door.

August tears himself away from me running a hand through his hair, face flushed and bewildered when the door swings open. Missing the feel of his body against mine, I whimper and clamp my hand between my thighs trying to fight the need building inside me like a storm brewing.

A tall handsome man with dark hair and honey-colored eyes strides into the room with a charming smile on his face. He's wearing a suit, and as he pulls his tie loose my eyes are drawn to his large, strong hands. A small part of my brain is bewildered at why a man like this, Loren I think April said he was called, would need to drug a woman to have sex with them. He was a walking poster boy for a CEO romance, so why choose a kidnap victim. How sick was he to get his kicks this way? Was he into something kinky? Was I going to come through this night in one piece?

"Ohhh, she is a beauty," he breathes with a hint of an accent as he kneels on the bed to stroke my face. Up this close I can see a small scar by his eyebrow, his olive skin smelling like sandalwood and the sea. *"Bellissima..."*

It's like an out-of-body experience as I arch into his touch and yet I'm disgusted with myself. I don't want him, I want August. Where is he? A shadow moves out of the corner of my but I'm consumed with sensation. I feel like I'm drowning in forced desire, my want is out of control and I hate the way it makes me feel. I rub myself against the sheets, as the Italian moves his hands up my thighs, to my hips where he strips away my leggings and my panties. He tosses them aside and my head is hazy as I whimper and moan, my wanton noises filling the room.

"So eager," He whispers before planting a kiss on my

stomach. He makes quick work of my t-shirt and bra, and all too quickly and yet not quick enough I'm naked.

When my step-father stripped me down and took everything from me, I was able to close off my mind. I pretended that I was someone else, somewhere else while hands dug into my skin and lips burned my flesh. Here there was no escape, the drugs made it feel like there was liquid sloshing around inside my skull, but I couldn't escape. I was trapped here, in my body, in this room, feeling everything as fingers pull at my skin.

"August," I beg, grinding the word out while I still have a hold on my sanity, a fat tear rolling down my cheek. "August..."

Finally, August steps back into view and out of the shadows, as the man between my thighs chuckles.

"I never realized you'd be watching August, you never did before," Loren teases as he leans back and unbuttons his shirt. "You like this one, huh?"

His words worm their way through the fog that's wrapped itself around me. How many times had August done this before? How many women had they taken? How many had gotten close to him, only to have him hide in the darkness? Was the affection he'd shown me all fake?

Loren massages my legs, parting them as his trousers

scratch against my skin. "Let me guess, daddy won't let you play with the flowers?"

His shirt joins my clothes on the floor, swiftly followed by his trousers and as he forces my legs further apart, I groan at the delicious burn that works its way down my thighs. There was something about the pain of being stretched that brought me back to myself and out of the haze a little more.

The stranger runs his fingers down my slit, where I know I'm soaked and smears my juices over my lips with a little groan of his own.

"God, the stuff you make here is potent," he murmurs in appreciation before bending and licking along the same path. Using his thumb to spread me, he thrusts his tongue inside my pussy, before flicking it roughly over my clit. My body is overstimulated, on the precipice of crumbling and with even the lightest touch from Loren, I'm a trembling mess.

"More," I demand, no longer caring about who is touching me as long as someone is. "More."

He obliges, feasting on me as he rips an orgasm from the body that is both mine, and yet not since I can barely control it.

Wiping his mouth he grins, reaching down and wrapping a hand around my neck as he thrusts into me. Curling my toes, I beg for more of his weight on me, more pressure but to my frustration his movements are slowly and leisurely.

"You know, I've never been one to follow rules...what about the three of us having a little fun?" He pounds me, but his eyes are locked on August, who watched with fury on his face. He's just as powerless as I am here and he knows it.

Tweaking my nipple with his free hand, he gives my breast a hard squeeze. "How badly do you want her? How far are you willing to go?"

His hips pistoning into me are driving me wild, as I reach up and scratch his back, silently pleading for more, he just laughs in response. My body seems to exist on a razor's edge, where it's all too much and not enough, which makes me want to cry and I'm vaguely aware that my cheeks are damp, maybe I already am crying?

Abruptly he pulls out of me, turning away and stalking towards August. Holding his cock proudly, I can see my wetness glinting off him in the low lighting. "Suck her juices off me, and if you make me cum, I'll let you be the one who fills that sweet little cunt up. That's what you want, isn't it?"

The brain haze doesn't ease up, neither does the burning lust, so I groan and wriggle into the bedsheets, pulling the pillow between my legs searching for something to ease the hunger.

"August," I sob again. I need him. I need him now.

August

The way Lilac cries my name as she tries to burrow into the sheets sucks the air from my lungs and before I can even register what I'm doing, I get down onto my knees in front of Loren. There isn't anything I wouldn't do for her if it was in my power.

"What a good little guard dog," Loren chuckles as he thrusts a hand in my hair and pushes my face into his crotch, he grunts as the traces of Lilac leave a sticky trail on my cheek and my forehead as he rubs against me.

"Suck it," he commands and I open my mouth, barely getting the chance to prepare myself before he thrusts. He's relentless chasing his own pleasure, skull fucking me without a second thought to my needs as I gag and dribble, spit running down my chin.

I'm conscious of Lilac moaning my name behind him, calling out for me in a desperate haze. I'd never seen it first hand, what happened during the germination phases, not up close and personal like this. I usually just helped the girls to their rooms and left, occasionally bringing up food and water. It was more unnerving than I thought it would be, watching her trapped inside her body, lost inside her head in a forced horny blur of sensations and emotions.

She sobs again as Loren makes me gag, grunting 'Fuck! Fuck!' with every violent push forward. I need Loren to come so I can focus on taking care of her, so without overthinking I massage his balls before moving a finger to his ass and applying a little pressure, without entering him. I've barely counted to five when he fills my mouth with hot spunk. As soon as I feel him spurt, bitterness flooding my mouth, I try to move away but his grasp on my hair keeps me pressed into him, my nose tickled by his pubes as I fight back the urge to throw up.

"Shhhhhhhh, *Angelo*." He murmurs as he strokes my face with his thumb before finally letting me go. Rushing for the washstand I spit, shooting him a glare over my shoulder. With another little laugh, he hands me a bottle of water from a stash that someone had brought up earlier, and I rinse. I watch as he takes a bottle of chilled white wine and a glass from the same box.

"Enjoy her, you've earned it." Taking a seat in the armchair near the fireplace, he leans back, relaxed, legs spread as he pours himself a large glass of wine. His eyes are fixed on us, and I know that the respite he's granting us is only temporary. When he feels like joining in again, I'll have no option but to let him or give in to his demands in the hopes that he's more interested in me this evening than Lilac.

These little events normally lasted the length of a long weekend, often with multiple partners depending on how much my father was being paid or who had the most valuable favors to barter. Luckily April had done Lilac a kindness, assigning her Loren since he didn't normally like to share his girls, which meant I didn't have to worry about another man tomorrow. If I can get her through until dawn, then that's one night down and only two more to worry about. I know that when this is over, she won't look at me the same way, with the same easy smiles but in the moment what choice did we have?

"Auggie, I believe your sweet little Lilac needs you."

Carefully, I sit beside her on the bed, stroking the hair away from her face as I offer her some water. She whines, eyes wild as she glares, obviously frustrated. I'm unprepared when she launches herself at me, tearing at my clothes, laying kisses on any areas of skin her mouth can reach.

"Off. Take. It. Off." She hisses, pulling my t-shirt up.

I quickly strip, which is no easy feat when Lilac is

pasted to my body as though she's afraid I'll turn into a puff of smoke and vanish through her fingers. Somehow, we manage it and she climbs into my lap, straddling my hips. She makes little moans and huffs as her hips move of their own violation, and she rubs against me.

Cupping my face, she stares into my eyes and for a moment I almost think she's lucid. Softly she presses her lips to mine, and it's like our roles are reversed as I'm the one pulling her deeper into me, needing more. She tastes like honey and sunshine, all warmth and sweetness. I can't remember the last time I enjoyed a kiss, with April it was always a way of asserting her dominance over me and keeping me under her control. I was beginning to recognize that her love for me was a weapon, and the threat of losing it was what kept me bound to her for so long. Lilac makes no promises, no threats, she just gives.

Her ass rubs against my erection, and a guttural groan is drawn from me as her hands move down my back, mapping every ridge, every muscle as though she was trying to read me like I was braille. There are no nails. No pain. Only gentleness. Kindness. Love. It feels like she's cocooning me in her desire and I never want it to end.

I squeeze her breasts, relishing the way she breathes my name before bowing my head to taste her. How did she always manage to taste sinful and sweet? Like a descendant treat, that I knew would eventually block my arteries and kill me. Flicking my tongue over the dusky pink buds, I reach up and roll the other nipple between my fingers, loving the way it makes her arch into me, gasping for more.

Threading her hands into my hair, she guides me back to her mouth where she kisses me like a woman possessed. She coaxes little noises from me that I've never made before. Is this what it feels like to be in love? To be wanted as I am?

"August, make me forget." She whispers before nipping at my earlobe and grinding down on cock.

"Mine," I promise, throat protesting as I grab my dick and position it so she can ease herself onto me. I feel as though I could see fireworks behind my eyelids if I shut my eyes, but I didn't dare, not wanting to miss a single second of Lilac like this. When she's seated, taking all of me into her tight warmth, we both groan against each other before deepening our kiss.

"I need you," she cries as she begins rocking her hips, bucking wildly chasing another release. Her hands are still on my face, holding me in place while I bring my hand up to grab the back of her neck, the other one, reaching between us to lightly brush over her clit with every glorious roll of her body.

"August. August. August," she simpers with every exhale and I want to freeze this moment. I want to remember it forever.

"G-g-got you." The words are murmured against the column of her neck as I feel her body clench and spasm around mine and she comes with an almost feral mewl. As she rides out the last waves of her orgasm, I wrap my arm around her waist and thrust up into her which has her tilting her head back and moaning my name as her tight body sends me over the edge, milking my cock mercilessly.

With each spurt of come, I thrust harder, as if I could somehow push it deeper inside her. I needed the only seed to take tonight to be mine. I wanted her. I needed to breed her. I needed to fill her up so that I was always with her. I wanted her to be able to feel me, sloshing around inside her. She was mine.

Pressing her forehead against mine, we pant and clutch each other tightly, until our breathing levels out and she buries her head in the crook of my neck. I hold her like this for a while, my dick still buried inside her, her legs wrapped around my waist. She seems to doze, lost to the world but the respite doesn't last long before she's hit again with a fresh wave of lust. Father had been working on his little concoctions for over thirty years, and he was particularly proud of this little aphrodisiac.

She tenses in my arms, as though her body was cramping before she lifts and thrusts down on me, using our combined releases as a lubricant. Her teeth scrape against the curve of my neck as she tries to fight against the drugs.

"Fast, August. Fast and hard," she snarls, fingers digging into my skin as she begs me with her body.

I swallow her demands, kissing her until she's fucking herself on my cock with abandon, not caring that I'm not yet fully hard.

"Such an eager little flower," Loren says appreciatively. His presence reminded me that I needed to keep her sated and calm.

Without ceremony, I flip her over onto her stomach, grab her hips and yank her ass into the air. If she wanted hard and fast, I would give it to her. Only me. All of me.

Pushing back into me, hips swaying she fists the bedsheets. "Yesssssssss."

The sound of flesh slapping together fills the room as I thrust back into her, the scent of sex permeating everything as we're consumed by a need for one another. Refractory period? What refractory period? She is mine. I need to make sure she understands that, I want her to feel it all the way down into her toes. When she wakes from the haze, I want her only to remember the way I made her body and not that way it all came about. Was that too much to ask?

I bite down her spine, overwhelming her with my touch, using my fingers to knead her skin. I wanted to flood her with feelings, the way I do when she smiles at me. Sliding my hand around her neck, I squeeze, compressing her airway as she clenches tighter around my cock with a cry. She squirms beneath me as she comes again, body hypersensitive thanks to the drugs, but I keep pounding her relentlessly until I feel a familiar tightening in my balls. Even though I'd already cum earlier, there was something about fucking Lilac that made me want to drain myself dry. I would twist myself into knots, wringing out every last drop for her if I could. With a growl, I come and collapse on top of her, placing gentle kisses over her shoulders and down her back.

With a murmur, words I can't make out, she rolls and pulls me into a cuddle, spooning her small frame as she passes out exhausted. I barely lift my head as Loren climbs into the larger bed behind me, his foot pressed against mine but his hands he keeps to himself.

When Lilac wakes with a fresh wave of need, both Loren and I satisfy her in the darkness. She takes him into her mouth while wrapping her legs around my waist as I fuck her until she's trembling. When Lilac stops shaking, body going still after yet another orgasm, I bring a bottle of water to her lips and encourage her to drink as Loren chuckles from the armchair by the fire. Finally, we coax her back to sleep, with Loren's cum drying on her face and mine spilling between her thighs. The last dregs of the drug would be making their way out of her system by now and as she falls into a deep sleep, I stroke her hair and pray that this is the end.

Loren climbs back between the sheets, "If I knew you fucked like that, we could have done this years ago, August my boy."

I'm not a boy, the pretentious wanker is the same age as me. I growl in response. I never wanted any of the others. They never meant anything and I cultivated, germinated and harvested them without batting an eyelid. She was my exception. I needed to protect her, to keep her safe to make sure she bloomed again and again for me. Tucking her into the sheets, I commit this image to memory. Lilac asleep, twisted in the bedsheets, smelling like sex and me is everything I could want. She looks peaceful, the weariness that lines her face vanishes as she relaxes into my warmth. She wakes twice more before the sunrises and we find ways to keep her occupied and blissed out.

She curls up into the crook of my arm, her head on my chest and I realize that I love her. There is no way I can let her stay here without talking to Father first. I don't want anyone else touching her. I allow Loren, only because it's the only way I can guarantee I'm the only one to breed her. The only sprout she'll grow will be mine. Tainted or not.

I slip from the bed, Lilac not stirring while Loren cracks one lazy eye open before deciding I'm not worth the fuss this early in the morning. As quietly as I can, I leave the room, grabbing my clothes as I tiptoe out.

I hide in the kitchen making a few phone calls, beginning to pull some strings together to weave an escape plan. If I could get Lilac out of here, stow her away, then I could keep her for a little longer. I know it wouldn't be forever, people like me don't get that kind of ending in life, but even a few more months would be worth it. Hanging up, I shove my phone into a drawer and jot down some details, folding the sheet up and tucking that away too.

I wonder if Lilac is awake yet as I climb the stairs two at a time, and just as I turn to re-enter the room, I spot April sitting outside my bedroom door, cigarette drooping between her lips.

"Where have you been?" Her eyes narrow and I know she doesn't expect an answer. She knows where I was last night. What I was doing. My room is next door and the walls aren't exactly soundproof. It's why her eyes blaze at me, and her eyebrows are pinched together.

I open my mouth, but like usual, the words don't come. I don't want them to. Why should I have to justify myself? Pushing herself to her feet, I can feel the anger rolling off her in waves. I was hers, I always had been. Poor sickly, weak little August, only good for grunt work and warming April's bed. Except...I wasn't. Lilac made me feel like I was more than that.

A yawning noise interrupts us, cutting through the building tension. "Relax April, I invited your brother to join in but he refused. He just watched like the good little pet he is."

Loren leans against Lilac's door frame, pants slung low on his hips, buttons open revealing a thatch of dark pubes.

April rolls her eyes, "Father's going to be furious if you've done anything to fuck this up."

Her words shouldn't scare me, but there's an edge to them that makes my heart rate pick up. He would hurt her just to punish me. He would harvest Lilac early because as much as he cherished his garden, he never saw the point in nurturing the weak flowers. They took up too much space and fought the strong for sunlight and water.

"Only if you tell him." Loren steps forward and

swipes April's cigarette out from between her lips. He takes a lazy drag before exhaling a plume of smoke lazily. Fucking Italians. "August didn't compromise the process so I don't see why you've got your panties in a twist. Jealous, *Tesoro?*"

April bristles. She was so used to being top dog and running the show, that when the investors and other florists came and she was relegated to simply being Aster Bramwell's daughter, there were moments like this. She would scratch, bite and lash out whenever she had the opportunity to flex.

"Fuck you, Loren," April growls in response.

CHAPTER SIX

Lilac

When I wake up, August is gone and Loren is tucked in my bed, snoring softly under the sheets. I turn my head and spot Loren's shoes tucked by my door and a small bag has appeared on my dressing table. He's going to share my bed all weekend, whether I welcome him or not.

The fog from my head is gone, my mouth feeling dry and furry as I swallow. Finally working up the courage to sit up I whimper at the heaviness of my limbs. My body feels used and abused, not in a painful way, but in the way you might overdo it after an intensive gym session. Last night August had done everything he could to make me feel...safe. Loved almost. My mind and my heart are at war about him, and the longer I stay here, the more he digs himself beneath my skin the harder it will be to rip out his roots. My freedom will demand that I break him, that I make him choose. I just wish it wasn't going to hurt me in the process.

He sneaks back into the room trying to be stealthy but when he notices me awake, sitting on the edge of the bed he flinches. I must look awful. I'm covered in sweat and bodily fluids, I don't even want to look at my hair because I know there's dried cum in it, causing it to clump together in big fat knots.

"Can I maybe shower? I'm feeling a little...grimy." I offer him a small, and what I hope is a reassuring smile. My foster father used to punish me afterward, if I was 'too miserable' or 'grumpy' and although I know August is not Kevin or Brody or Mike, it's a risk I don't need to take. I need to keep him happy and make him trust me.

August nods and offers a hand to help me stand, I stumble a little, my legs weak and I don't miss the way the top of his ears turn red. Was he blushing because he was proud of what he'd done or because he was ashamed, or was it both?

August was too tender towards me to feel like a threat, but the men in my life who'd been like that had always been the worst. I thought they'd protect me, care for me and then all they did was take.

The hot water washes away what feels like a layer of dirt and sex, and as it swirls down the plughole, I feel invigorated. Focusing on the heavy droplets running down my body and wiping clean my sins gives me time to process last night.

August wasn't the one who drugged me, he could have stopped it though. Shaking my head, I scold myself for thinking that way. If he'd stopped me from drinking the wine, I would have had to endure everything stone-cold sober. If he'd intervened, April would have been cruel with her punishments on purpose.

She hated me, but I also seemed to amuse her. She was torn between wanting to braid my hair and rip it out, leaving my scalp bloody and raw. Clearly, that was weighing on her every time she looked at me. If we'd met in another time or place, I'd swear that she was just a lonely woman who had no idea how to make friends. But then August had fallen into his obsession with me and that had swung the pendulum towards the hate side of her emotions.

Memories of last night flood my brain as I use the washcloth across my stomach, down over my hips and between my legs. Loren had faded into the background, his pleasure, his words, even his face was faded, hazy thanks to whatever it was they gave me. August, however, burned brightly in my thoughts. His mossy green eyes never left my face, his intensity sending shivers up my spine. I'd heard about people eating with their eyes, and when August looked at me like he had last night I felt consumed, devoured until there was nothing but crumbs left behind.

It's the same way he watches me now, as he stands against the doorway of the wet room. The house is eerily silent, everyone still in their rooms, the staff pottering about quietly so as not to disturb them. It feels like a private moment, this shower, just between the two of us and for some reason that makes my skin warm.

Last night I wasn't myself, my body and my mind were uninhibited, desperate shadows of the real me. My choices were taken away, my autonomy brushed aside like peat that had fallen out of the flower bed.

But here? Now? Now, I was in control of everything. I wanted to touch August, kiss him, make him moan in that strangled, raspy voice of his. I wanted to do things without anything else influencing me.

I reach out and grab his t-shirt, pulling him under the spray with me. He's perplexed, his face scrunched up as he glances around as if I'm about to play some sort of trick on him. It isn't until I'm peeling off his soaked t-shirt that he realizes my intentions and practically shoves me out of the way as he reaches across to turn the water off.

My fingers fumble slightly as I undo the button on his jeans and push them down his thighs. With one hand snaking its way up his chest and around the nape of his neck, I pull him down to me and kiss him as though he was my oxygen, the very reason for my existence.

He tastes like mint and longing, and as he presses closer into me, I know he's just as hungry for my affection as he is my body. My other hand wraps around his cock, his arousal evident as I feel it pulse and twitch at the contact. With a firm grip, I give him a leisurely pump, loving the way his hips jerk in a little aborted thrust as a soft noise leaves his lips.

Taking my time, I squeeze before stroking him again. He nips at my bottom lip as I swipe my thumb through the bead of pre-cum forming at the head of his dick. If dicks could be considered pretty, this would be one of the prettiest I'd ever seen. It was thick and hard with a slight curve and the tip, slick with pre-cum looking almost like a glistening shade of pink. I continue to rub him, teasing him with unhurried motions as we devour one another. I'm offering myself to him, willingly and I see the moment he recognizes it for what it is. A gift.

"Lila," He murmurs against my lips, our breaths mingling in a hot mess of need. The C of my birth name still escapes him, and I like him better like this, eyes glazed over with lust, mouth hungry for me, body aching to be touched by me.

His hands begin exploring my body, cupping my breasts, brushing a thumb over my nipples. His touches are light, soft, loving as if he's afraid to hurt me after last night. I ache, and I probably shouldn't want this as much as I do, but I'm not some fragile thing. Everything else has been taken from me, and this is the only thing I can control right now at this moment. And that means something to me.

His right hand dips lower on my body, as he brushes his thick fingers over my wet lips, before sliding a finger tentatively inside me, gauging if I'm in pain. I arch my back, pushing my hip towards him, demanding more and with a chuckle against my neck, he slides another finger inside me and uses his thumb to massage my clit.

"Mine. Lila, mine." He rasps against my skin as he plants kisses over my shoulder, across my collar bone and up my neck. Even though it causes him pain to speak, with every syllable dragged up his raw throat falling from his mouth, I understand that it's his gift to me in return.

His capable hands work me into a frenzy, and although I was the one in control when we started this, I'm well aware that I'm now whimpering into his chest as he pushes my body closer and closer to the precipice. I can feel every nerve in my body being wound tighter and tighter like a coil ready to spring and he's unrelenting, never changing pace just steadily pushing me over the crest.

When it feels like I'm about to burst out of my skin, all of my muscles taut, he applies a little more pressure, and like an egg, I shatter into a million pieces with a choked back sob and shudder as my body clenches and spasms around fingers, my hungry pussy demanding more.

Smiling up at him from under my lashes, he looks positively sinful with his jeans still around his thighs, but his t-shirt discarded. I stroke his face before turning around and placing my palms against the cool tile, my ass pushed out. He reaches out and squeezes my cheeks, kneading and caressing them before he lines his thick cock up against me and thrusts into me with a feral moan. A hand comes up, into my hair and he yanks me backward, forcing my back to arch as he kisses me over my shoulder, all the while pounding into me. He rolls his hips and I can't stop the whimpers that I make, even if I wanted to. The noises we make reverberate around the tiled wet room, sounding even filthier as he takes what he needs from my body.

I can hear little huffs against my shoulder with each thrust and I think he's whispering 'mine' to himself as he pulls out and slams back in so hard I'm almost convinced he'll break my spine. I can tell when he's close, because he loses all sense of rhythm, his body acting on instinct as he chases after his own orgasm. With a grunt and a final thrust, he drapes his sweaty body over mine as I feel him spurt hot liquid inside me, his cock twitching and his fingers digging into my hips. If he didn't love me before, he does now.

When he pulls out and turns the shower back on, his face looks softer, more tender. Without saying anything else, because he doesn't need to, he strips off his jeans, grabs the washcloth and helps me clean myself for the second time that day. It's unhurried, considerate and almost reverent, the way he touches my body. We stand, kissing under the water like we have all the time in the world, like we aren't in the house of horrors, being bred for a complex and confusing human trafficking ring. Like we aren't pawns in his father's game, just two lovers, enjoying a shower together before the rest of the world wakes.

"Mr. Bramwell is looking for you," A meek voice calls from the doorway and I spot one of the staff wringing her hands nervously as she stares at her feet.

August startles a little as if it's unusual for his father to ask for him and it just confirms what I already know. He strokes my cheek and motions for me to stay put, probably knowing that his father wouldn't keep him long because he didn't care for August. I nod, even though I know this may be my only opportunity to find out about The Harvest and their plans for me. This might be the only chance I get to escape before they put a baby in me.

A baby. That's a whole other complication I don't know how to deal with right now. I wasn't prepared for a child, I hadn't planned on having one any time soon but hearing that I would and it was going to be taken away made me feel like something was twisting up inside my chest. Painful, sharp stabs right under my ribs and for a moment I pretend it isn't happening. I imagine that I met August in a normal way, maybe at a coffee shop or while out at a bar. Inside my head, I pretend that we plan to have a baby, both of us choosing and enjoying the journey together. And then what? We live happily ever after in a quaint house, nestled away in the suburbs? Try as I might, I can't imagine having a life with August beyond having a baby, because my thoughts turn nasty and I envisage him taking away our child and forcing them into a life like this. Fighting the bitterness that has crept in, I quickly dry myself and pull my yoga pants and baggy vest on.

"You think you're so fucking special," April grinds out, her nostrils flaring as she watches me with cold eyes.

I don't reply, knowing that she's looking for a reason to punish me and if I speak, I'll be giving her ammunition that will be used to break me. Bowing my head, I clutch my towel in my fist and stare down at my bare feet. Shows of submission can usually calm her, but today that doesn't work, probably because I'm covered in August's marks.

"Father should have just left you chained up in the caverns like they used to," She snaps as she grabs my elbow and starts directing me towards breakfast. "I mean, August and I came from a crop that never saw the daylight after they were cultivated, well...until they were moved into the nursery, and we're just fine."

My brain ticks over her words and instead of answers I find more questions. They were 'sprouts' themselves? And their crop...flowers...mothers, were kept in those dingy cave-like rooms until they gave birth? Who raised them? What happened to their mothers? I hadn't seen any other siblings or children here, only staff, security and their creepy father who was too nice to be genuine. They grew up alone, only with each other in this fucked up garden of hell.

I grab some fruit from the breakfast buffet as we sit at the table, ignoring the flinty looks she keeps throwing at me. Her cruelty had always been there, simmering away, boiling over when one of us angered her so I don't know why I felt it more today.

"Fine?" I snort quietly as I cut my apple into slices, "You're fucking your brother."

My words come out louder than I planned and I flinch as she barks out a short laugh. I don't know why I said that, I know better. I'd grown up being taught when to keep my mouth shut, I was well versed in submission for survival, but her statements were like thorns under my skin, scratching and poking and I couldn't ignore them.

Shrugging she stabs her knife into a grapefruit. "I doubt we're biologically related. So many men come through these doors to spread their seed."

My foggy memories conjure images of Loren saying something similar the night before as he fucked my mouth, about how he'd requested me for the whole weekend and August should be grateful since it made it easier on him to not have to share me with multiple men.

April looks sly now, as if she can see into my mind and that Cheshire cat grin returns, "I mean you've been fucked by two already and we're only a day in. How many do you think will have spunked inside you by the end of the week Lilac? Ten? Fifteen? More? I bet you can take all that dick like a champ."

Her words cut through me, and I recall similar phrases uttered in my teenage years by men I was supposed to trust. Swallowing, I brush aside the memories, refusing to cower under the weight of them. I would survive this, just like I survived that. I would take this whole thing, pack it into one of my pouches and tuck it away. I would move on. I would be free. The shame and crippling self-worth issues that had begun to wrap themselves around my limbs fade as I inhale and exhale carefully. Managing my breaths until I felt more in control.

"You'll get yours, weed. Nothing lives forever in The Arboretum and The Harvests are coming." April continues as she bites into her bitter fruit, tearing the soft pink flesh away from the peel as the sharp juice trickles down her chin.

"What's The Second Harvest?" I understood that The First Harvest or simply The Harvest was when they were going to cut the baby out of me and sell it to the highest bidder, but what was the second one? What was worse than being used as an incubator for nine months?

Smirking, April leans back in her chair. "You'll find out. Just stay away from The Greenhouse if you know what's good for you."

When she looks relaxed and smug like this, I have to fight back the urge to punch her, because I know it will only end up worse for me. Her obvious dislike for me grows every day, and while she'd never had to beat me or cut out my tongue, I couldn't be sure she wouldn't do those things now out of spite.

There's something about her words that almost sound like she's baiting me, and before I can stop myself, I find myself asking, "Do you think I'm stealing August away—is that what this is? Afraid of being replaced, April?"

She tosses the rest of her grapefruit down onto the plate, lip curled. "Like I already said, you won't be here long. August was grown here, he'll wither here too and return to the soil with me as it should be."

August

A fter changing into some dry clothes, I grab my phone and my scrap of paper from earlier, stuffing them into my pockets before I go in search of my father. It's approaching nine but the house is mostly silent, everyone too spent from the night before.

Father's dinner parties are legendary, and not just for the flowers. We usually only have three or four seedings at one time, and Father likes to invite twelve or so florists, nursery workers and horticulturists for his weekend celebrations. Now, even he recognizes that the flowers can become exhausted and overwhelmed, so he organizes activities, invites some high-class escorts and breaks out his magic mushroom stash amongst other things. It's a weekend of debauchery, and he does this twice a month until they become pregnant, filling the weekdays and the other two remaining weekends with a more regular partner for the soon-to-be flowers. And when I say more regular bed partner, I mean whoever is willing to pay or contribute the most to my father's empire.

I knock on my father's office door and quietly let myself in. He'd always been an early riser, and especially when the other florists came to visit since he was the congenial host, providing a warm bed, quality whiskey and florals of the rare kind.

"August?" He frowns and scratches at his temple for a moment before sighing. "Since you're here, I might as well discuss Lilac with you."

He puts down his pen and pushes aside the paperwork he was looking at when I entered. I wasn't privy to the business side of The Arboretum, since April would take that over someday and I was just here to assist. I cultivated the flowers, kept them in line and helped with the harvests. In our family hierarchy, I was on the bottom rung, a general dog's body and until now, that had always been fine with me.

My father clears his throat a little before linking his fingers together and raising his chin so that his face tilts up at me, "April thinks she may be becoming a little bit of a... distraction for you."

Hissing, I look down at my still bare feet. I knew it was only a matter of time before April betrayed me. I should have known that she couldn't stand aside for nine months until The First Harvest. She was not a patient creature.

Narrowing his eyes at me, his voice becomes stern, all his usual charm evaporating. "I've seen the way you watch her boy, like a starving wolf eyeing up my chickens and I cannot allow that. You are a failed strain; a weak specimen and you need to remember that."

I remember it. I remember it with every cut or bruise. With every transfusion. I remember it with every painful swallow and every lost word. When he took away my voice, it was to remind me that I was broken, to keep me chained to him as a silent pet. I'd had infusions all my life and they helped, but it wasn't enough when he'd poured whatever he was working on at the time down my throat, he thought I would die choking on my own blood. And I almost did. April saved me, calling for an ambulance the second he'd hit me during our fight before forcing water down my neck to wash away anything that lingered. She told them about my condition and so by the time he'd picked up the beaker, grabbed my face and begun pouring, the emergency services were already coming through the front door and heading towards The Greenhouse. I should have died. Even with my clotting medication. They saved my life. But what a life I've lived since.

The repair operations afterward, all the care I needed, only served to confirm to my father that I was nothing but a weed, unfit for his flowerbeds. April is the reason he allowed me to stay. He knows I'm her anchor, he designed it that way.

"After Loren is finished with her, I will take over as

her breeder. She is my flower after all. It is my responsibility to see that she blossoms and reaches her full potential."

I clench my fists at the thought of my father touching Lilac, breeding her, raising her child. No, I would not let him. I would free her. I'd stolen her away before, I could do it again. She was mine.

He carries on, oblivious to the plans I'm making in my head. "It's been a while since we kept a sprout on-site since they are such hard work, but it might be worth thinking about the next generation. April is nearing thirty and she will need a protegee the way she has been mine."

I watch as he stands, and moves with that fucking cane of his to the window, where he looks out across his plantation and strokes the end of his mustache thoughtfully. The corner of his mouth pulls up, into a smirk that is so reminiscent of April's it makes the hair on my arms rise. "Lilac is pliant, sweet-natured and, according to Loren, a fantastic partner to plant with. Perhaps I should marry her instead, make her care for me in my old age"

Now I know he is taunting me, reminding me that I am nothing to him. He doesn't seem to realize that Lilac looks at me like I'm her everything. The sweet smiles, the gentle touches, the way she gives herself to me willingly without drugs or violence—I would kill to keep those in my life. He won't have her. I won't let him.

Biting back the rage I can feel simmering away in my stomach and threatening to spill up my throat, I nod curtly.

"I actually have some tasks for you today, so April will take over your garden duties and help your flower rest."

He hands me a sheaf of paper with a list of addresses in the city and orders of death blooms from the last harvest. Crumpling the paper in my fist I nod again. I would run his little errands, but only because I had a few things of my own to do and this way I wouldn't have to find an excuse to go into town. With a wave of his hand, he dismisses me, returning to his posturing at the window without another glance in my direction.

I make my way over to The Greenhouse and ask Jeff, one of the nursery workers, for the keys to a delivery truck and watch as he and the others load up the orders. The Arboretum had regular delivery drivers for the standard produce, but for the death blooms, delivery was entrusted to one of the nursery workers, April or myself. The process that it took to cultivate, germinate and bloom them meant that father rarely trusted anyone else with them since they were his responsibility right up until they were signed for.

Casting an eye over the flowerbeds, the ones hidden behind the sheets that Lilac was so eager to explore, I wonder why she is so different from them. Why didn't I want to help any of them? Why wasn't I drawn to them? Was it because they cried? Because she never did. Even after last night. Even when Rose lost her tongue or Poppy was punished in front of her. She shed tears of desperation while under the drugs, but that wasn't the same. That wasn't fear-induced. She never looked at me like she hated me...that must be it.

When I was a boy, I used to help my father dig the flowerbeds, we would turn the soil over, adding the bonemeal carefully. When I was a teenager, I began to help prepare the bone meal itself, the bones needed to be stripped of any flesh or muscle, cleaned and then steamed before it was ground into a fine powder. Bone meal was essential for helping the plants grow larger, and Father said it created a more plentiful crop, but I still hated the mess it made. Only the weakest flowers were used for the bone meal, the others were replanted for The Second Harvest.

The First Harvest was the hardest, it required the most preparation and dedication. The Second Harvest was easy. They weren't even conscious for most of it, and it was kinder that way. I hope none of them were aware because I understand all too well what it's like to be trapped, helpless and without a voice.

"All done, Auggie," Jeff calls with a shout and a small wave. I nod to let him know I've heard him before climbing into the refrigerated delivery truck and setting up my GPS.

My body feels like there's electricity running over my skin, am I nervous? Is it because I know I'm about to betray my family for Lilac? She could be carrying my child, I could have a family of my own with her. Wasn't that worth fighting for? A sense of foreboding settles in my stomach like a rock, and I resolve to get this trip into the city over with as quickly as I can and then put my plan for escape into action. I wouldn't share her with Loren for any longer than I had to, and I would cut off my father's hand before he even laid a finger on her soft, creamy skin. But first, I had to deliver the death blooms.

CHAPTER SEVEN

Lilac

April looks up from her phone, a bored expression on her face. "August is out on a delivery, he won't return until later. Try not to get into too much trouble without him."

With that, she stands and leaves the table. When she doesn't return, a nervousness settles over me. Why had she left me alone? Did she think I posed no risk at all? Were her words about The Greenhouse a warning, or were they meant to tempt me? I peel the skin off an apple slice, playing with the fruit until it starts to turn brown at the edges before deciding that this is my only chance. If April punishes me for it later, at least I'll know what The Second Harvest is and how I might be able to avoid it.

The house is still quiet as I wander out towards the back porch, down the steps and across the garden. As I enter the plant nursery and my eyes adjust to the low lighting with the windows mostly covered, it dawns on me why August kept me away. Looking over the medical beds, each containing obviously pregnant women, I understand why they call this the nursery. The only actual plants in here are some plotted ones dotted around the room, instead, it's like a medical ward.

This was The First Harvest. Bile rises up my throat as I creep closer for another look, unsure if the women were sleeping or drugged. No one moves or even stirs as I approach, and given the way their eyes seem to twitch beneath the lids I'm going with drugs. The screens beep, filling the air with a rhythmic noise as these women seem to have fallen into a synced pattern. Clearly 'Father' doesn't think they're likely to wake up any time soon given how there are no nursery workers or security placed here.

When I reach a woman with a significantly smaller, slightly flatter stomach, I pull back the sheet. Lifting her gown I can see an incision into her skin, cleaving her open from hip to hip, I assume so they could remove her child. The gash has been stapled neatly back up, and she is clearly being looked after since her vitals seem similar to the other women around her and the cut shows no signs of infection. Grabbing her chart, another wave of nausea hits me. *Daisy Goldblum. 2003. B negative.* She was eighteen. Did her family miss her? Did they think she was dead? Or did they assume she'd run away? I gently stroke her dark hair, offering her comfort I know she can't feel, tears beginning to roll down my cheeks. Fuck. I move along to the next bed. *Heather Bronson. 2001. O negative.* And the next. *Ivy Garcia. 1997. A negative.* And the next bed again. *Holly Davis. 1999. AB positive.*

All flowers plucked and stolen, ripped up by the roots like I was. Their babies would be harvested soon too, what would happen when they woke up? What was the last thing they remembered? This was what awaited Poppy, Rose and me if we became pregnant. We would be drugged and hooked up to machines while they waited for us to become ripe, so they could bust us open like a fucking coconut.

Unable to hold it back any longer, I drop down into a crouch, my arms around my knees as I cry. And cry. And suffocate on my own sobs, forgetting how to breathe as I mourn these girls. I don't know how to help them. I don't know how to save them and I know I told myself the guilt could wait, but it's like a dam has been broken and there's no fighting the emotions flooding me. How could I forget where I was? Even for a moment in the showers with a tortured man with the saddest green eyes I've ever seen. How could I forget who he was? I shift forward onto my hands and knees, throwing up on the concrete floor. Slowly I regain control over myself and push myself back onto my feet.

Quickly I start pulling all the wires out of the machines, ignoring the way they bleat loudly as I do until eventually, they all fall silent. As carefully as I can, I also remove the IV drips, tearing in to the bags and letting the solutions pour across the floor. I might have just killed them, Daisy, Ivy, Heather and Holly. I might have just extinguished their only hope of survival, but was living worth it when you woke up to an empty womb and at the whims of a crazy old gardener? When everything was stolen from you, was death a kindness? I rock back on my heels, the weight of my actions hitting me full force as I look at their still bodies.

Strong hands come around my waist and drag me backward. A sharp sting in my neck makes me cry out, thrashing against the large broad body that has me pinned, a flash of dark hair and a square jawline tells me it's Lars who's crushing me to him like I'm nothing more than a pillow. I open my mouth to scream, to call for August before I remember he's not here. The edges of my vision go blurry as I wriggle and squirm, trying and failing to find a way to escape but it's no use.

As my world fades into blackness, I hear Father whisper in my ear, "It's a shame, you would have produced an excellent quality sprout. Instead, we must move onto The Second Harvest."

The evening sun filters in through the glass, casting rainbows around and for a moment, I feel relaxed, my limbs loose and floaty. It's only when my brain registers where I am that I fight the restraints pinning me to what appears to be a dentist's chair. The Greenhouse is beautiful in the daylight, filled with pretty hues of green and bright bold colors and the flowers preen in the warmth but at night everything is shrouded in darkness. The orange glow of the setting sun doesn't fill me with warmth, instead it reminds me of blood as it cascades across the greenery.

Glancing around I realize I'm behind the tarpaulin sheets, the ones August had warned me about. Three of the walls are lined with huge raised flower beds, filled with dark, rich soil and standing about 3 feet tall. Two of the beds seem to be hooked up to more wires, and some sort of water system as multiple IV bags hang on a rail that runs parallel to the beds. They're also the only ones with anything growing, with three markers in each bed making it six in total as the third flower bed appears empty. I'm in the center of this strange semi-circle of sorts, in the stupid dentist chair, and beside me there are what look like medical supplies on a wheeled trolley and a comfy armchair that seems oddly out of place. Lars stands to one side, April sits behind him, perched on the edge of a flower bed and Father paces around the chair, tapping his cane on the ground with each step walking in slow circles that make my eyes hurt trying to watch him.

"I don't understand," I croak, swallowing carefully. If the sun was setting, that meant I had been here all day and as feeling slowly returned to my body, I felt stiff and sore.

Father pauses in his pacing, "My wife was the first flower I'd ever planted. She was barren you see, something we didn't realize until we'd been married over three years. So, I helped her, I allowed her to create life the only way I knew how."

He talks as if what he's saying is common sense, but my brain can't process his words. My head throbs steadily as some of the haze lifts. If the whole day has passed, where is August? Does he know I'm here?

Father leans over and strokes the petals of some of the tulips growing from the beds. The petals are a rich deep red color that reminds me of wine or blood. "The flowers that bloomed from her were divine. Rich in color, vibrant and the scent was unmatched. It was like eating fresh fruit, succulent juices sticky on my face when I'd previously only devoured tinned imitations."

He chuckles to himself, and even April smiles tightly. Where was her grin now? Was she feeling guilty over goading me into exploring? Did she realize how angry August was going to be when he returned?

"I'm still a scientist at heart dear Lilac, so of course I use my own pain and heartache to experiment with the process." He strolls in front of me again and I hate how refined he looks. His three-piece suit is immaculate, not a crease or a speck of dirt anywhere. It's no wonder he's easily able to hide what he does here when he looks like an upstanding gentleman who wouldn't hurt a fly. His fake charm makes my stomach roll in protest.

He carries on talking and I'm struck by how much he loves the sound of his own voice. Maybe that's why he took away Augusts? "If an infertile husk of a woman could grow the most beautiful blooms, then what could a young fertile body produce? That is how my death blooms were born."

Flowers? Infertile wife? What? Was he saying he grew them out of her grave? I glance between April and Lars, but their faces are impassive as if they've heard this story hundreds of times.

"Over the years I've perfected our technique to get the most out of the experience. We care for you, keep you in optimal condition and it pays off with the harvests." He stops near the empty flower bed and rakes his hand through the mud, the way you might with sand at the beach as if he were drawing shapes in it. "We're currently experimenting on whether death itself can make the flower bloom more poignant. More..."

"I don't understand..." I repeat, my tongue is like lead in my mouth. It feels too heavy, too dry, too big. Can you choke on your own tongue? Father looks across at me, his eyes narrowed, irritation flashing.

He speaks slowly, choosing his words carefully as he takes a seat in the armchair and crosses one leg over the other and rests his hands, one on top of the other, resting on his cane. "I used to open up the flowers, crack them like a chestnut, fill them with soil, surround them with it and let them grow. But they were already gone, already cold and decaying. Cold shells, that spark of life squashed out."

April nods in agreement as she stands and stretches. She takes up her father's habit of pacing, now slowly strolling around the flowerbeds, gently touching each plant marker as she goes.

"So, I worked on ways to keep them fresh. Warm." He smiles and this isn't a congenial, false, oozing with charisma kind of smile. It's real. And cold. And self-satisfied. "They infuse their life into the death blooms in preparation for The Second Harvest. It's why The Arboretum only produces the finest flowers. It's why we sell them for thousands of dollars. We invest in the process, and it pays dividends in the end."

Now I'm fully aware, and it's like I can feel every nerve in my body as my limbs protest at being tied down. My head's clear and I play back his words carefully, he grew flowers with his dead wife, but it wasn't enough...so he was choosing girls to infuse his blooms with what? Life? Death? The moment in between?

The tubes. The wires. The six species markers poking out of the soil. I feel sick as I spit out the words, "You mean...you bury them? Alive?"

Leaning back into his armchair, Father seems pleased that I've finally grasped his twisted business model. "We create the best environment for the flowers to bloom. And of course, regular monitoring and watering allow me to continue developing the process. Growth is continual, Lilac. Progress is not a stagnant pool, it is an ever-flowing river, carving a path into the soil."

"I don't...I don't understand..." I'm sobbing again. Six markers. Three in the nursery. Two in the house and me. That's twelve. Twelve lives he's stolen and crushed beneath his heel. Twelve women who did nothing wrong except having the misfortune of being born with floral fucking names.

Where is August? Does he know about this? Did he realize that this was what they were going to do to me nine months from now? The tears fell faster, of course he did. He was the one who plucked me. Was his affection just an act? A game he played with April? If that was true, that would be beyond brutal. Maybe April wasn't always the cruelest one...

"Hmmm, how can I simplify this for you?" Father stands and moves to the closest flower bed. Where the bunch of red tulips are growing, proud and tall, he points proudly, "It is a form of xeriscaping in a way. Willow here has been given antibiotics, and a hydrating electrolyte solution to sustain her."

He shifts slightly to point at the next marker, golden yellow and orange chrysanthemums burst from the soil in a splash of color. "Jasmine has only been given water,"

He points over to where purple geraniums are beginning to bloom, "And Dahlia over there has antibiotics and the minimum amount of water."

I writhe against the bindings, my pain more than just physical. My soul hurts. I'd had a hard life, I knew suffering and struggle. But Poppy certainly didn't, Rose had never been broken before and I was willing to bet the others were just as sweet and kind, still figuring their lives out. Father was a monster. A cruel, savage, selfish monster who was taking the good out of the world so that he could grow some fucking daisies.

"Are they conscious?" I snarled through my distress, watching the soil carefully as if I expect a hand to pop out zombie-style.

Shrugging, he looks thoughtful for a moment. "Barely. They do not need to be conscious and in fact, we prefer that they aren't to minimize the distress. Like meat, it might affect the quality of the product if they are tense and scared."

I don't miss the way he says barely, that's not a definitive no. So, they could be awake and aware under that dirt, just trapped in their bodies because of whatever shit he's pumping into them. He motions to April, who turns a dial on a console on the wall and slow, steady *bah-dum, bah-dum, dah-dums* fill the room. My ears strain against the mix of noises, and I can pick out two more beats besides the original one, so at least three of them are still alive under there.

"We do care about them, Lilac. The same way we care about you." Reaching out he strokes my hair, the same way I had for Daisy back at The Nursery.

"Father, let's hurry this up. Your guests are up at the house waiting for you to join the revelries," April interrupts, cutting off his lies before he can spout any more.

Father didn't care about anyone but himself, that was clear. He killed his own wife and made her into plant food essentially. The Second Harvest is when they pick the flowers from the soil that you're buried in. The soil they stuff inside your chest cavity or your c-section scar. The mud you slowly suffocate to death in. Those were his death blooms.

"What're you going to do with me?" I don't know why I ask, because I know what the answer is going to be. He's going to stick me in the mud, so I don't destroy his little empire. He's going to hide me away until I rot.

"We're going to use you as another test subject. If we inject you with a serum April has been working on, we might be able to use your harvest as a control group." Father sounds serious as if he's logging everything in his head to type up a report later.

"And then you'll bury me alive?"

"I'll make sure you stay alive for as long as possible, Lilac, don't you worry about that." April practically hums as she inserts a cannula into my arm near the crook of my elbow. "I can't promise it will be pain-free though after the chaos you caused in The Nursery."

Father nods his head, "Ahhhh yes. The Nursery. Don't fear, Lilac. The current crop is all fine and back to being monitored safely."

I hope for their sake those girls aren't in any pain and never wake up. Where is August? Why isn't he here? For a moment, I miss him.

Watching April as she hooks up a bag to my drip, working quickly like she's done this hundreds of times before, my stomach clenches as I wonder how many people have sat in this chair. My world once again dims, and it's like there's cotton stuffed into my ears as my senses are dulled.

There's a loud crash, and then somewhere I hear someone roar, "No! MINE!" The words echo around The Greenhouse and as my eyes flutter shut, I know he's come for me. My monster.

August

I knew something was wrong when I arrived back at the house and I could hear the music and cheering from the driveway. Father's gatherings were always loud and energetic, but he had more class than to let it morph into a frat party which is what it feels like as I watch one of the escorts streaks across the grass in a thong, chased by a tree expert I recognize as having flown in from Sweden.

Pushing my way inside, I stride past the drunken men and women enjoying themselves on all the furniture and look for Lilac. There's no sign of her. I call April, but it goes straight to voicemail. I can't spot her either.

Moments later Loren bumps into me, grabbing my arm firmly. "Where've you been? Where's the flower? I've been pretty lonely without you."

Casting a glance at the pretty blonde hanging off him, I turn back and raise a brow. I don't need words to be able to convey the fact that I don't believe him.

"I'd rather be with you two. Where is she?" He says suggestively, looking around me for Lilac. But if she's not with Loren, like she's supposed to be then that must mean she's still with April. The same April who isn't answering her phone and is feeling territorial over our relationship.

Why does my chest feel tight over the thought that the two of them are missing, while I can find Poppy and Rose easily amongst the guests? Neither of them is where they're supposed to be and it sets off alarm bells inside my head. I dash up the stairs but find both bedrooms empty and when a staff member tells me that my father is also absent, I know exactly where I'll find them.

I race out of the house and into the gardens when I hear shouts of 'Fire! Fire!' behind me. Turning, I spot Rose clambering through a window to the side of the house, climbing over the porch railing and sprinting into the tree line. If it was any other night, I'd attempt to stop her but things were different now. She wanted her freedom, she'd fought for it and I wouldn't take it from her again. People are spilling from the house as flames begin to lick up the side, and I take that as my sign to go and find Lilac. I didn't give a shit if everyone else got out alive, only her.

Entering The Greenhouse as quietly as I can, I march straight through to the cordoned-off area. I know what's hidden behind here, I always have, but I wasn't ready for Lilac to see. I didn't want her to have to face this, not when there was a chance I could save her from it. For a moment I think I'm too late when I see her strapped to the chair, eyes closed, chest barely moving as her breathing slowed.

"No! MINE!" I scream with everything I have, trying to get my father's attention. He needed to realize I was serious about Lilac, and I would do anything to save her from being harvested. I bellow again, even though the pain in my throat makes my eyes water.

April glances up, dropping her hold on the IV bag and I see the guilt flicker across her features before jealousy rears its ugly head.

"Here to save your little plaything?" She scoffs, mouth twisted into a nasty smirk.

"Not a... plaything. Mine." I rasp, my eyes burning into hers. I need her to know that I am not backing down on this. All my life I have bent to April's will, she was my savior, my friend, my sister. Now, as she stands there preparing to cut into what's mine, she's the enemy.

My father sits in his armchair, watching like a king overseeing his gladiators preparing to battle each other. He says nothing, but he doesn't intervene either, clearly eager for whatever is about to happen.

April rolls her eyes as if I'm a child and she's done with my petty games. "I don't have time for this. Lars, hold him. He's going to watch as I slice her open and pack her with dirt and seeds.

Lars approaches me and I warn him off with a growl but it's no use, he still moves closer arms outstretched. We grapple, pushing and shoving one another before I finally grab his wrist, twisting him until I have his arm pinned up his back. That doesn't stop him as he tries to kick out, twisting in an attempt to free himself. With as much force as I can muster, I slam my foot down on his leg until I hear his tibia crunch and give way. Lars drops to the floor like a sack of potatoes and I wince. I considered him a friend, but he was just another reminder of how nothing in my life was really mine.

"Stop being foolish, boy and stand aside." My father commands with a dismissive wave of his hand. The noise from the house gets louder, my father tilting his head as screams of 'FIRE!' fill the greenhouse. He jumps to his feet alarmed, face marred with concern but I know it's not for the risk to human life, but for his paperwork and his plants should it spread.

"House burning down," I say, a smile pulling at the corners of my mouth.

"I have more important things to worry about than this flower April, kill her and be done with it. I need to check on the house." He heads towards the exit, but I block his way. He needs to understand that Lilac will be leaving here. Alive and in one piece.

The look he gives me is withering, that is, if I cared about what he thought anymore. I don't move, matching his stare with one of my own. Still, I say nothing and I stand firm. The smell of smoke starts to permeate the air, a sign that the fire is spreading outside. Maybe it's already reached the vineyard? Or perhaps The Nursery is ablaze?

With an exaggerated sigh that seems to say 'Look what you're going to make me do!' he twists the head of his pretentious cane, unsheathing a sword stick. "Move August. Or I will be forced to hurt you too."

His dark eyes are flat as if he couldn't care less whether he stabbed me, only that I was an inconvenience he could do without.

"No," I growl, crossing my arms, ignoring the way Lars is still moaning on the floor in a heap behind me, trying to secure his leg and slow the blood loss.

Father lunges, sword aimed at my chest but I step aside and shove him to the floor as he passes me. He turns, blade swiping out and narrowly missing my ribs. I shoulder barge him, sending him crashing into one of the flower beds, and he has to reach out to stop himself from toppling face-first into it. He dives for me but I throw out my elbow, and there's a pulpy crack followed by a gush of blood as my father's nose is broken.

Cupping his face with one hand to try and stem the bleeding, Father groans and whimpers like a cornered animal. I allow myself to relax a little, waiting to see what his next move will be and not even a minute passes before he strikes again, this time for my neck. He wasn't trying to warn me, he was trying to kill me.

I force him away, grabbing his wrist and slamming it against the wall until his fingers unclenched and the sword falls from his hand, landing on the floor with a clanging noise. He swings a fist and catches my cheek, making my head snap back but it doesn't stop me. I won't let it. Not when I have so much to lose. Grabbing the lapels of his suit, I hold him tightening in my grip before thrusting my head forward into his. His eyes roll in his head, and I use that as my opportunity to headbutt him again and this time his eyes shutter closed and he slides down onto the floor.

"August! Have you gone crazy?" April screams as rushes over to check that Father is still breathing.

Ignoring her I rush to Lilac's side, relieved when I see the steady rise and fall of her chest. It doesn't look like they'd gone much further than putting her to sleep, so I quickly undo the bindings that keep her pinned to the chair before reaching for the cannula in her arm.

"I won't let you ruin this August!" April seethes as she tries to push me away.

Disregarding her, I rip out the IV tube, wishing I could have done it gently, but April is clawing at my arms trying to stop me, her nails cutting into my skin. Ruby red droplets begin forming before they trickle down my arm and onto the floor. She wasn't done taking her pound of flesh from me, even after all these years but this would be the last time.

We tussle before I manage to shove her away, buying myself a few seconds to try and rouse Lilac. April clambers onto my back from behind, biting into my neck as I reach behind me to grab a fistful of her hair. Using my hold on her, I manage to wrench her free and hold her at arm's length while I shake Lilac again.

Her eyelashes flutter and just as I think her eyes might open, April twists herself out of my grip and tackles me, arms firmly around my waist as she knocks us both to the ground. For a moment I lay there, dazed, my head thumping and the smell of smoke getting stronger.

"Why? Why would you do this for her?" April spits as she tries to pin me down.

"August?" A quiet voice calls, and we both turn to see Lilac watching us with a confused expression and heavy-lidded eyes.

I force April off me and push myself to my feet, kicking out at my sister as she tries to grab my ankles.

"Is there a fire?" Lilac asks sleepily as she tries to sit up but slumps back down into the chair. Glancing over my shoulder I see tendrils of black smoke beginning to creep under the tarpaulin sheets, which means that most of the estate must be consumed by now. It would only be a matter of minutes before the flames managed to find a way inside The Greenhouse and then I would lose Lilac anyway. I couldn't have that. She deserved to live. She needed to be free.

"Here," I dig in my pocket and hand Lilac the keys for the delivery truck parked in the drive, my mobile and the scrap of paper from earlier. "Take."

"What's this for?" She sits up again, this time managing to stay upright as she begins to get to her feet.

"Your freedom," I murmured against her hair, inhaling the soft scent of lilacs.

"August..." Her hand cups my cheek seconds before she pulls me down into a kiss. Our mouths come together hungrily as if this is the last time we'll ever get the chance to do this and it registers in my head, that it is. I'll miss the way she tastes, the way she feels in my arms, the way she moans my name. She makes me feel like I'm the only person in the universe who matters, and I knew when I first kissed her when I first touched her that I would never be able to keep this feeling. She was a butterfly, and my life here would crush her. My family would pin her in a pretty little box and display her on a wall just to torment me if I stayed with her.

"Love you, Lila." My words get lodged in my throat, and now because of the scarring but because I've realized and accepted that my escape plan has one fundamental flaw. I will never be able to leave here. Leave them. But she can, and I can give her that.

"I love you too," she murmurs against my lips before she's pulled away, dragged backward by her hair by a furious April.

"I never should have let you live. I should have gutted you the second he started looking at you with hearts in his eyes!" April's voice cracks and I know she's hurting too. The whole family is tainted. We're all toxic, right down to the roots.

Stepping towards them, I ignore the orange light casting around the room and the tendrils of smoke creeping ever closer. I ignore my father stirring against the wall or how Lars has managed to drag himself out of here and is now God-knows-where. My focus is on the only two women who I have ever loved and who love me, even though the difference is like night and day.

"Let her go, April," I growl, lunging for them. I don't know how, but I manage to tear Lilac from my sister's grip and shove her towards the side door. The temperature in the room increases and I know if I look behind the sheets, I'll see flames. It was now or never for Lilac.

"Run!" I hiss, but Lilac pauses.

"What about you? Come with me! I can't leave you!" She cries, tears streaming down her cheek as she looks at my father, who's covered in blood and unconscious, April who looks feral and me, damaged and bleeding. She pauses, imploring me with her eyes, begging me to come with her hand outstretched. But I can't.

April runs at her, but I hook my arm around her waist and swing her, holding her against my chest. I can hear the crackle of flames now and if Lilac doesn't leave soon, we'll all burn here.

"NOW LILA!" My screaming has an effect since she knows how much it hurts me to speak louder than a whisper and she turns and runs for the door, glancing back with tears streaming down her face before vanishing into the smoky night.

Shoving her head back, April manages to give me a nosebleed that won't stop streaming but thankfully doesn't feel broken. As I drop my hold on her and stagger backward, she pushes me to the floor and forces me onto my hands. With one of her sharp knees on my spine, April has me pinned as she straddles my back, keeping one arm behind me like I'd done to Lars, my other hand trapped underneath the weight of us both. Rocking my hips, I manage to gain a little leverage and buck upwards, which unseats her. It only lasts for a few moments but that's all I need to free my left hand, which shoots out and grabs my father's sword stick before April even realizes what I've done.

Using my limited freedom, I roll, taking her with me and as we move, I slide the sword through her shoulder, using it to pin her down. It cuts into her skin easily, especially with my weight behind it and as I look down into her snarling face, I'm filled with a whirl of emotions I can't explain. I feel guilty because this is April trapped beneath me with a blade in her shoulder, keeping her fixed to the floor. I did that to her. I'm the reason she's writhing in pain. But also anger. She never should have put me in this position. Sadness is also present, although it's only a sliver fading fast as April hisses curse words.

"It's meant to be us. It's always been us." She sobs when she realizes I'm not going to let her go, squirming to pull something out of her pocket. Reaching down with one hand, I stroke her face. We'd been through so much that we'd grown twisted and destructive.

"It shouldn't...have been. He...stole everything. He made us...like this." My words sink in and it's like a heaviness settles over us both as her body relaxes beneath me.

I can smell burning plastic now as one of the tarpaulin sheets catches fire, the flames angrily spreading around us as ruining everything my father ever held dear. Everything is suffocating, the heat from the blaze, the weight of my love for Lilac, my family's expectations and The Arboretum. It's time to let it all go.

"Love you, Auggie." April pulls my head down to rest against hers like we'd done so many times before. It was how we'd comforted one another. How we centered ourselves in the wilderness of The Arboretum. A droplet of sweat trickles down my head and lands on her cheek, blending in with her tears as we hold each other, bleeding and broken.

I barely feel the sharp pinch in my side as she slides her pocket knife between my ribs. I'm not surprised, in fact I'd expected it to end like this when I woke up this morning and started plotting my escape. After all, the villains can never have a happy ending, life doesn't work like that.

Whispering, I kiss her forehead, "I know.

EPILOGUE

I t had been almost eight months since my life had changed. Since I was plucked from the street, cultivated like some sort of rare seed and planted in that depraved, fucked up place. There was nothing left of The Arboretum now, just charred remains and barren land since the fire had ravaged everything. All the foliage had provided fuel for the flames until it consumed every last shrub. The burnt-out framework of the house looked like it could be knocked over with a strong gust, and as I drove past it for the final time, I prayed for a storm.

The news reported that several bodies had been recovered but were damaged beyond recognition but the house owner was considered to be one of them since he had otherwise vanished. They had mourned the loss of leading horticulturist Aster Bramwell, the man I'd only ever been introduced to as Father. The tragedy also claimed the life of his only (known) living child, April even though her remains were never identified either and just like that, August was written out of the public records. Even in death, they've managed to isolate him, and if I allow myself to dwell on that thought for too long, tears gather.

When August had told me to run, to find the provisions, I assumed I'd be looking for a car, or maybe a cell phone, a stash of food and a handful of cash to just get us out of there. Instead, I'd found keys to a safety deposit box inside the delivery truck, with a note giving me directions and telling me that if we were to be separated to meet him there.

Well, I drove to the box. He'd stashed away almost $250,000 in cash and another $50,000 in bonds. I waited, booking into a grimy motel in the city, opposite the bank. And then I waited. I waited for almost a month before I got the message that he wasn't coming. He hadn't made it.

I know Stockholm syndrome is a very real thing, I'd seen Beauty and the Beast as a child too. I could never forget that he'd taken me, that he was part of the whole twisted setup...But then I think about how they treated him. How he was a perpetrator but also another victim. Another harvested flower that had been used and abused by the people who were supposed to care for him and my heart feels like it's cracking inside my chest with the contradictions of it all.

They were gone.

And I was free.

That was all that should matter.

I used the money to find somewhere to put down roots. Just a small two-bedroom house out in the suburbs of a town three states away. I hadn't wanted to risk running to anyone who might have survived, and it always lingered in the back of my mind that they might have made it. Their bodies were never formally identified and The Arboretum was built upon skeletons. It would be an easy feat for one of them to fake their death, and so I lived constantly checking over my shoulder for the first three months. I soon settled as I found my place in my new town, and made friends with my neighbors who I knew would look out for me.

"Looking good Mrs. Stevens!" Emily from next door calls over the fence as I reach my front gate. She's a lovely fifteen-year-old who loves basketball and is learning to play the violin, badly I might add. Since my bump had ballooned in the last two months, she was always kind enough to compliment me whenever she saw me, which was every day.

"Thank you, Em! How was school today?"

"'Urgh, boring, she groans just before her mother calls her in to help with her younger brother.

My neighbor from the other side, an older woman called Sharon, stops by my front gate and holds it open for me. "Lyra, do you need me to send John over later to cut the grass? I really don't think you should tackle it in your condition."

I changed my name to give me a layer of protection but also to start my life over fresh. I was no longer Lilac Oakridge. Or Lila Johnston. I was Lyra Stevens, the widowed young wife of a soldier who moved to start her life over and live quietly with her baby. The baby that served as my only reminder of August and not for the first time, I wonder if it will have his mossy green eyes and golden colored hair. We never could have had a happy ending—he was too damaged, done too many unforgivable things and I knew that. I told myself that I didn't love him. I couldn't, I was just using him to escape captivity. But when the nights are long and cold, I curl up in the dark and miss the feel of his hand on my cheek or the warmth of his presence.

I take a few waddling steps forward, unwilling to dwell on the loneliness that sometimes catches in my throat, instead rubbing a hand over my large belly as I balance my shopping on my hip in a brown bag. "That would be lovely!"

As I approach my front porch, my shopping bag falls from my grip, tins and cartons clattering to the floor with a thud.

"Is everything okay? Is it the baby?" I hear Sharon ask, voice laced with concern.

I can't breathe. It's like the air has been sucked out of my lungs as I take a step forward, trembling hand outstretched. On the steps of my porch in a washed-out jelly jar, are a bunch of lilacs tied in a purple ribbon.

The End

Acknowledgments

J as always, thank you for picking up the domestic slack so I can focus on my writing. Chonky and Dog, my constant companions throughout – I would have finished it sooner if you hadn't wanted so much fuss.

Ash, Raven and Heather, your feedback helped me shape this into something I could be happy with. Thank you for telling me like it is and giving me some great suggestions.

I wouldn't have finished this without Ally, Glenna, Sian, Andi, Kessily, Abrianna and Niki. The writing sprints with you guys kept me on track and sane, so thank you!

About the Author

Alice La Roux is a dirty minded, mouthy Welsh author who is still trying to find her genre while dabbling in erotica, fantasy and horror. She owes her husband, best friend and sister everything—without them she wouldn't be writing. She's a bookworm who reads anything and everything and is addicted to social media. If you want to stay in touch and get the latest updates (or just see pictures of her dog) then don't forget to stalk her!

Check out her links below and you can also follow her on TikTok: @alicelaroux

facebook.com/asmadasAlice

instagram.com/alicelaroux

ALSO BY
Alice La Roux

Firebird

Two's Company

Sinclair

Master

Addicted to Love

The Good Girl

Also coming in 2021

Queen of Hearts

Survival Games written under the name AJ Everheart

TAG

Hide & Seek

Printed in Dunstable, United Kingdom